The Army Doctor's Christmas Baby

Helen Scott Taylor

Other Books in the Army Doctor's Series

#1 The Army Doctor's Baby

#2 The Army Doctor's Wedding

The right of Helen Scott Taylor to be identified as the author of this work has been asserted by her in accordance with the UK Copyright, Designs and Patents Act, 1988.

This is a work of fiction. All the characters in this book have no existence outside the imagination of the author, and have no relation whatsoever to anyone bearing the same name or names. Any resemblance to actual events, locales, or persons, living or dead, is purely coincidental.

Acknowledgments

Thanks go to my wonderful critique partner Mona Risk who is always there when I need her help, to my son Peter Taylor for creating a gorgeous book cover, and, as always, to my reliable editor Pam Berehulke.

Chapter One

The taxi pulled up outside a quaint thatched pub with twinkling Christmas lights strung along the eaves and around the mullioned windows. Kelly Grace hugged her long fleece coat tighter over her scanty clothing. On this cold winter's evening the place looked welcoming, but the last thing she wanted to do was go inside. She had made a huge mistake.

"I can't do this," she said to her best friend, Maj. Cameron Knight. He and his wife, Alice, were crammed in the back of the taxi with her.

"Come on, Kell, you promised," Cameron said.

She hadn't promised, but in a moment of weakness she had agreed to deliver a singing telegram to one of Cameron's friends at his birthday party.

Now she had cold feet. In fact, in the skimpy bunny girl outfit she had cold everything. She'd worked for a singing telegram service when she was a student. Back then, walking into a room full of strangers in a weird costume hadn't bothered her. Ten years later she wasn't as confident, even after a glass of wine to bolster her courage.

"You look lovely, Kelly," Alice said with a smile, understanding Kelly's fears although Cameron was plainly oblivious.

Cameron handed some cash to the taxi driver and

1

reached across Kelly to open the door. "Let's hurry. I don't know how long Sean will stay. It wasn't easy persuading him to come. I want him to have a bit of fun tonight. He works so hard, he deserves it."

"Hey." Kelly dug in her heels and stayed put. "What do you mean by fun? I agreed to sing 'Happy Birthday' and give the man a quick kiss. That's all."

"I know. But you'll hang around and chat with him, won't you?"

"Yes. If he wants me to. But I'm not an escort service."

"I didn't mean to make you uncomfortable." Cameron looked mortified.

Alice giggled. "I can't imagine Sean needs help getting a date if he wants one."

"He told me he doesn't have time to date," Cameron said. "But every man needs female company occasionally. He's a nice guy, Kell. I think the two of you will hit it off. I only want you both to be happy."

Cameron was matchmaking. Kelly almost laughed at the irony. She opened the car door and stepped out into the freezing cold. Tiny specks of ice swirled in the wind, stinging her exposed lower legs. She shivered. This was not a night to be clad in nothing but fishnet pantyhose, stilettos, and a black swimsuit. Oh, and bunny ears; how could she forget those?

Cameron slid out behind her, circled the vehicle, and helped his very pregnant wife to stand and carry the cake box. Alice was normally small and delicate, but right now her belly was nearly as round as she was tall. She must be uncomfortable, but Kelly would swap places with her in a heartbeat. Alice had everything Kelly longed for—an adorable toddler, a baby due any day, and Cameron.

Kelly's breath rushed out in a smoky plume of regret and sadness. She turned away from the sight of the man she loved with his arm curved protectively around his wife as he helped her cross the slippery car park.

A burst of warm air fragrant with the smell of wood smoke and cooking met Kelly as she pushed open the pub door and stepped into the cozy interior. A log fire crackled in the hearth and low oak beams decorated with horse brasses crisscrossed the ceiling. In the corner, a modern silver and purple Christmas tree looked as out of place as Kelly felt. She hesitated and waited for Cameron and Alice to catch up.

"Where's the birthday boy?" she asked.

"His name's Sean."

"I know." She'd heard of Col. Sean Fabian; all the army doctors and nurses she worked with had. He and Cameron's brother had designed battlefield protocols for treating serious trauma that were used by military medics across the globe. She'd partly agreed to this crazy scheme because she wanted a look at the army's famous plastic surgeon.

Cameron took the cake from his wife and stepped past Kelly. "Sean's in the other bar. He'll be easy to spot. He's the only guy with blond hair." He set the box on the polished oak bar and pulled out the cake. "Let's put the candles on, then Alice and I'll go in. Give us a few minutes before you follow with the cake."

"Fine." Kelly kept her coat buttoned, acutely aware of the men in the bar eyeing her fishnet-clad legs.

Alice held out a hand. "Let me take care of your purse for you."

Kelly handed it over. "Thanks."

"Sean really is a nice guy," Alice said. "Don't be put off by his looks."

"What's the matter with him?"

"Nothing, believe me. Nothing at all." Alice gave an enigmatic smile before waddling across the room towards the lounge bar. Meanwhile, Cameron had pushed five candles in the chocolate icing and lit them.

"There you go. All ready." His lips quirked in a

3

mischievous grin. "Do I get a sneak peak at the bunny girl outfit?"

"No. You'll see it soon enough." Kelly shoved him in the direction Alice had gone. "Go and make sure your wife is comfortable."

"Yes, ma'am." He saluted and headed across the room. "Don't be long," he threw over his shoulder as he left.

The tiny candles atop the cake splintered into starbursts of light as sudden tears filled Kelly's eyes. Now that she'd left the army, she would miss Cameron so much. The thought of never working with him again twisted a painful knot in her chest.

A corner of Kelly's heart would always belong to Cameron, but she liked Alice and wished them only good things. Still, she had put off telling Cameron that she'd resigned from the army. When she did, he was bound to ask questions she didn't want to answer.

Unbuttoning her coat, she pulled it off and hung it by the door, suddenly not caring who saw her in the skimpy outfit. What did it matter? In a few weeks she would be working for a charity, nursing poverty-stricken children in Somalia. It was unlikely she'd see any of the people here again for a long time.

She just had to get through the next few weeks. Christmas was a time for children and families, a tough time for her. She normally liked to be overseas in a field hospital somewhere.

Ignoring the blatant stares, she grabbed the cake and followed her friends. She needed to deliver it before the candles burned down to stubs in pools of wax, ruining the delicious chocolate icing Alice had made.

Kelly peered around the door into the crowded interior of the lounge bar. Groups of comfy sofas dotted the room and the hum of happy conversation filled the air. She spotted the army group standing by the bar and noticed the back of a blond man's head.

Cameron caught her gaze, grinned, and nodded.

"Happy birthday to you," she sang and stepped forward, holding the cake aloft. As one, the group turned and most joined in the song as if they had been expecting her.

Curious to meet this brilliant army doctor, she fixed her gaze on Col. Sean Fabian. As he met her gaze she stumbled, nearly dropping the cake, the familiar words to the song dying in her mouth. Oh my goodness! The man was stunning, his eyes an extraordinary aquamarine color, like nothing she'd ever seen before. Alice's strange comment about not being put off by his looks suddenly made sense. He was so good-looking, it was intimidating.

Kelly's cheeks heated with embarrassment—if only she'd taken a moment to check her makeup in the restroom when she arrived. Somehow she closed the distance between them and held out the cake.

"Happy birthday," she mumbled.

A grin kicked up the corners of his mouth. He gave her a crooked smile, dimples appearing in his cheeks, those incredible eyes sparkling with pleasure. Her stomach flipped and she struggled to draw in air. No way could she kiss *this* man in front of everyone. No way.

"Thank you very much. This looks delicious." His gaze flicked from the cake to her face as he took the chocolate confection and placed it on the bar.

"Kiss, kiss," Cameron chanted and some of the others joined in.

Although it would be embarrassing to kiss Sean, it would be more embarrassing to refuse. She really had no choice. Obviously a gentleman, he waited for her to make the first move.

Her high heels brought her eye to eye with him. In a dreamy daze, Kelly stepped forward, rested her hands on his lapels, and leaned in. His fingers gripped her waist, gentle yet firm. The wool of his jacket brushed her skin, making her feel vulnerable, wearing so little while he was fully dressed. He smelled delicious, spicy, with a hint of baby powder that squeezed her heart.

"I don't know your name," he whispered as if for her ears only.

"Kelly Grace." Her words were little more than a breath of sound as she leaned closer, his mouth mere inches from hers.

Her eyelids fell as their lips touched, barely a kiss, but enough to wipe her mind in a heady rush of sensation.

For the first time in seven years, she wanted to melt into the arms of a man who wasn't Cameron Knight.

Eyes closed, Sean inhaled Kelly's floral fragrance and flexed his fingers against her waist. His heart pounded as he pressed his lips to hers in a sweet kiss. He hadn't touched a woman since his wife, fearing any intimacy would rouse painful memories. Yet kissing Kelly was nothing like kissing Eleanor. There was a gentleness about Kelly that put him at ease.

Instinct demanded he draw her closer and kiss her properly, but a busy pub was not the place for that.

Opening his eyes, he took half a step back and reluctantly let his hands drop to his sides. Kelly glanced at him beneath her lashes then averted her gaze, somehow managing to appear demure even though she was dressed in little more than her underwear.

He shrugged off his jacket and settled it around her shoulders. Covering her up seemed silly, given the circumstances, but he sensed she was uncomfortable. "Is that better?" he asked softly as she adjusted the jacket swamping her slender form.

"Yes, thanks."

"I don't usually bother much about my birthday, but

you've made this one to remember. Would you like a glass of champagne?"

"That sounds great." She flashed him a smile, a hint of vulnerability in her warm brown eyes that made him want to wrap a protective arm around her. He settled for placing a hand on her back and easing closer to her side as he handed her a full glass.

Sean's younger brother, Daniel, grinned, giving him a thumbs-up. The bunny girl was the sort of entertainment Daniel would have booked, but as he'd flown in from New York a couple of hours ago, that was unlikely. The only other one of Sean's friends who'd pull a stunt like this was Cameron.

He checked Kelly had enough champagne, then touched her arm. "Excuse me a moment. I'll be right back."

He edged through the crowd and offered Cameron his hand. "Thanks, mate. That was a nice surprise."

Cameron shook his hand and slapped him on the back. "You're welcome. I thought you and Kelly Grace might hit it off. We've been stationed overseas together many times and she's a great girl."

So Kelly was an army medic. Sean glanced back at the beautiful woman, her thick mass of dark hair glinting with mahogany highlights, her shapely legs so long they seemed to go on forever. Sean might have found time to ask Kelly out, but he didn't date anyone he was likely to work with. His job at the military hospital was too important to risk compromising it in any way.

With a sigh of regret, he shouldered back through the crowd to her side. True to form, Daniel had moved in to flirt with her, his date scowling beside him. Sean gave his brother a hands-off look.

Daniel grinned, unabashed, and looped his arm around his date's waist. "Well, you're another year older, and I'm jet-lagged so I'd better head off and get some shut-eye. Are you coming to Mum and Dad's for Christmas?"

"Maybe. I'll see how it goes."

"In other words, no," Daniel said.

Sean shrugged. It was no secret that he and his father didn't get along. Ever since Sean left his father's exclusive cosmetic surgery clinic in London to join the army, relations had been chilly.

"Okay, well, I'll see you sometime over Christmas," Daniel said. "I want to see my two little nieces. I have lots of fun presents for them."

"You're welcome anytime. You know that." Daniel might have his faults, but Sean's twins, Zoe and Annabelle, adored him—probably because he was a big kid at heart.

Sean embraced his brother and gave a wry laugh when Daniel play-punched him in the stomach, catching him off guard.

"You're getting slow, old man. I thought you army guys had lightning-fast responses."

"The only thing I do lightning-fast these days is fall asleep when my head hits the pillow. Looking after two babies and working full time will do that for you." Not that he minded; his career and his girls were his life— they were all he needed. Or he'd thought they were until an attractive bunny girl walked into his life and woke up his libido.

He cast Kelly a longing glance as she sipped her champagne and smiled, appearing far more relaxed now Cameron had moved to her side. Kelly Grace was a beauty indeed, but even if she weren't out of bounds, Sean had his hands full with his girls and his job. He didn't want the extra complication of a woman in his life. He'd been there and done that. In his experience, women caused nothing but trouble and heartache.

"Are you sure you don't mind giving me a ride? I can

call a taxi." Kelly slipped her arms in her sleeves as Sean held up her coat.

"Of course I don't mind. The army housing is on my way home."

Kelly had planned to share a taxi home with Cameron and Alice but they'd rushed off to the hospital. Alice's back had started aching and she was worried the contractions had begun.

The cold nipped Kelly's face as she hurried across the car park beside Sean. He juggled the box, containing the remnants of his birthday cake, and a couple of wrapped presents as he fished in his jacket pocket for his car keys.

The locks popped on a silver SUV and he opened the door for her to climb in. The interior smelled of children, the blended fragrance of baby products that took her back seven years to her time working in pediatrics.

Sean jumped in beside her, dumping his cake and presents on the floor in the back before rubbing his hands together. "It's darned cold tonight. The forecast is for a white Christmas this year. I hope that's right. My girls will love the snow."

As Sean started the car and cranked up the heat, Kelly glanced over her shoulder at the two baby seats installed in the backseat.

"Cameron mentioned you have twins."

"I do, Zoe and Annabelle. They've just had their first birthday and they're into everything." He grinned, his eyes twinkling with pleasure in the streetlights. "They're the best thing that ever happened to me."

"You're very lucky." Everyone around Kelly seemed to be having children at the moment, as if fate insisted on taunting her with what she could never have.

They fell into a comfortable silence as the car headed along the narrow country lanes back towards Oxford. Headlights shone in Kelly's eyes. She blinked drowsily as the car warmed up.

"So, you're in the medical corps?" Sean asked.

"No, the nursing corps." Kelly fiddled with a coat button. "Actually, I resigned from the army awhile ago. I've nearly finished working out my notice period. I have leave until after Christmas, then I'll be back on Civvy Street."

She wasn't sure what made her tell a man she barely knew something she hadn't revealed to her best friends. Cocooned in the dark car with Sean, she felt strangely safe and relaxed. He had a polite manner and he was easy to be with. After months of wondering if she had done the right thing by resigning from the army, she felt at ease with her decision.

He flashed a curious glance her way before turning back to the road. "What do you plan to do now?"

"I was a pediatric nurse before I joined up. Something happened recently that made me realize how much I missed working with children." The face of the dear little African boy Cameron had adopted came to mind. One day of caring for that baby reminded her how much she missed her old job.

"I've given the army seven years of my life and gained a huge amount of experience that I'd never have had working in a civilian hospital. I want to put that knowledge to good use. I've decided to work for a children's charity."

"Nursing?"

"Of course. I'm due to fly out to Africa in the New Year. Conditions will be tough, but I'm used to working under pressure in conflict zones. There are so many children out there who need help. I want to be part of that effort."

"Sounds great, Kelly. I admire your principles." He fell silent again, his lips pressed together while his fingers tapped the steering wheel.

The car stopped at traffic lights, then turned beside

the building where her apartment was and drew to a halt.

Kelly picked up her purse and Sean swiveled in his seat to face her. "Do you have any plans for the next couple of weeks?"

"Not particularly. Why?" A streak of excitement burned away her drowsiness. Was he about to ask her out? She normally didn't like casual relationships, but Sean was so easy to be with. It would be nice to spend a little time with him before she left the country.

"The French au pair who usually looks after Zoe and Annabelle is going to stay with her family for Christmas. I planned to put the girls in the day care at the hospital while she's away, but I'd rather not. Every time they go in there they come back with colds. If you're free, it would be great if you could work for me for three weeks before you start your new job. I'll pay you, of course."

He wanted to employ her! Disappointment flashed through Kelly but soon vanished when she stopped to think about what he was offering—three weeks of caring for his twin girls.

"I'd love to." She pressed her hands to her cheeks, visions of all the things she and the two babies would do racing through her mind. This was going to be so much fun.

He grinned. "That's fantastic. I'm sure you'll hit it off just fine with my little monsters. Why don't you come over tomorrow and meet them while Monique is still here. She can run through everything with you. You can use Monique's room while she's away. It's next to the girls' bedroom."

"You want me to live in? Okay." Excitement bubbled inside Kelly. Instead of a lonely Christmas break on her own, she could spend it with Zoe and Annabelle. And Sean, of course, when he was at home.

"That's settled then. I'll give you the address and the

11

PIN code to get in the gate." He scribbled on a piece of paper and handed it across, then jumped out and came around to open her door.

She climbed out, grinning.

"It takes about thirty minutes from here. Come over tomorrow morning when you're ready. I'm there all day."

Kelly nodded, her head spinning with the sudden change in her plans. This just might be the best Christmas she'd had in years.

Chapter Two

The GPS on Kelly's phone directed her along a narrow country lane beside the River Thames to a set of tall iron gates. A metal sign that read RIVER VIEW HOUSE hung on the wall. She edged her car closer and tapped the PIN code Sean had given her into the keypad. The gates swung open to reveal a drive that cut across a neatly trimmed lawn.

Her car crunched along the gravel and around a corner. She stopped, catching her breath at the amazing place. For some reason she had expected Sean to live in a historic house like Cameron did, but this building was ultramodern with lots of huge glass windows, sandstone walls, and a slate roof. It sat on a hill above the River Thames. The views from the property must be fantastic.

In a parking area outside the front door stood the SUV Sean had driven the previous evening and a sports car. She pulled up beside them and cut her car engine.

Climbing out, she grabbed a breath of chilly air, locked her door, and surveyed the property. It really was a wonderful location, quiet and peaceful with beautiful views in all directions. This close to Oxford with a river frontage, the place must have cost a fortune, at least a couple of million pounds. A colonel's salary had to be a lot more than she'd thought, unless his family already had money. She really knew very little about Sean Fabian apart from his military reputation.

Her heart pounded as she walked towards the front door. She hadn't expected seeing Sean again to make her nervous. After all, she was only working for him. They weren't dating. She sucked in a steadying breath and told herself not to be so silly.

She pressed her thumb on the doorbell and waited. A few moments passed before voices sounded inside, then the door opened. Sean beamed his crooked smile at her, all dimples and white teeth.

A small girl with blonde curls rested in his arms, her head on his shoulder, her chubby fingers clutching his shirt collar. Kelly's heart skipped a beat, then raced on. If there was one thing better than a handsome man, it was a handsome man holding a baby. Or in Sean's case, two babies. The other twin sat on his foot, her arms and legs wrapped around his lower leg.

"Kelly. Hello. Great to see you again. Come in." Sean shuffled back, one foot weighed down by his daughter.

"This is Zoe," he said, bouncing the baby in his arms. He tried to sit the child higher so she could see Kelly, but the little girl buried her face in her daddy's neck and hung on. "We're slightly shy when we meet new people, but she won't take long to get used to you." He kissed the top of the child's head. "This is Kelly. She's going to spend some time with you while Monique's away."

"Hello, Zoe. It's nice to meet you."

The little girl peeped out at Kelly through huge blue-green eyes fringed with long golden lashes just like her father's.

"And down here we have Annabelle, or Belles for short." Sean lifted his foot off the ground and the child tipped back her head, viewing Kelly upside down. "As you can see, Belles is not shy. I think she takes after her mother and Zoe takes after me."

Kelly crouched down to Annabelle's level and

smiled. "Nice to meet you, Annabelle." The two little girls were identical twins, both blonde and very pretty.

"Annabelle has a thing about riding on my foot at the moment. It's like walking around the house with a lead boot on. By the end of the day, I feel as though my leg is going to drop off. I'm sure I'll end up with one thigh muscle twice the size of the other."

Kelly's gaze rose to his denim-clad thighs, exactly at her eye level. They looked pretty good from where she was crouched. She stood quickly, a flush heating her cheeks.

"I'm afraid Monique's already gone and there's a chance she won't come back. Her grandmother isn't well, and she took a turn for the worse. So I'll show you the ropes." Sean angled his head to talk to Zoe. "Shall we give Kelly a tour of the house?"

Zoe peered shyly at Kelly and nodded, poking a thumb in her mouth.

Kelly suppressed a smile as she followed Sean down a light, airy hallway. He limped along with Annabelle on his foot, obviously a doting father.

"The main living area is a semi-open plan to take advantage of the view."

A huge bright room lay before her, the front wall made up of sliding glass doors. As she'd suspected, the room had incredible views of the river and surrounding countryside.

Contemporary white leather sofas and easy chairs filled one section of the room, while an oak and stainless steel kitchen with a granite-topped island occupied one back corner and a semi-screened dining area with oak table and white leather chairs another.

Kelly wandered across the space and stared out as a boat drifted past. Wooden decking provided an outside seating area, elevated above the river. "This is a stunning view, Sean." She glanced over her shoulder as he shuffled closer, wincing at the weight of Annabelle on his foot.

"I love it here. I'm a bit of an introvert. I need to retreat somewhere peaceful after a busy day at work to recharge my batteries."

"Yeah, this place would be ideal for that." She didn't think of herself as an introvert, but she did like some quiet time alone after a hectic spell in the field hospital. Being an army medic could be incredibly stressful, often dealing with multiple cases of severe trauma in a short period of time.

Just because Sean was not overseas in a conflict zone didn't mean he was under any less pressure than she had been. The most severe trauma cases were shipped back to the hospital at Brize Norton for Sean to take care of with the help of Cameron's brother, Radley.

Day in, day out, Sean operated on the most severely injured service personnel from British army theaters of operation all over the world. That would put any surgeon under pressure.

"Let's go upstairs. I'll show you your room and where the twins sleep." He placed Zoe gently on the ground. "Come on, angel. Big girls walk on their own feet, don't they." She clung to his arm as he tried to let her go.

With difficulty, he lifted Annabelle up and stood her on her feet as well. She leaned back against his leg, staring up at Kelly beneath her lashes. Sean offered each child one of his hands and they toddled along beside him.

"They've been walking for a few weeks. It's a bit of a mixed blessing now they're more mobile. They can move like greased lightning when they want to. I need about ten hands sometimes."

"Well, you have two more now."

He glanced over his shoulder and she held up her own hands and wiggled her fingers.

His amused grin made her heart do a little jig. There

was something incredibly attractive about Sean Fabian and it wasn't just his handsome face. She liked him, really liked him. She would have to be careful not to forget she was only here to do a job.

They made slow progress up the stairs as the two little girls climbed on all fours in front of him. When they reached the top, they both dashed into a room and Sean followed. Kelly stopped in the doorway of what was obviously the nursery. A wooden crib was set on each side of the room and a baby changing unit sat against the glass sliding doors overlooking the river.

She would even have a lovely view when she changed the girls' diapers.

A colorful mat covered the main section of the polished wooden floor. Both girls sat down there and fished toys out of a toy box in the center.

Annabelle toddled over and held up a doll to Kelly. She was definitely the more confident twin.

"Thank you. What a pretty dolly. Is she yours?" Kelly kneeled and Annabelle sat on her lap.

"I seem to have made a friend," she said, glancing up at Sean.

"Zoe will take a little longer to accept you, but she'll get there. She takes time to trust people."

Sean sat cross-legged on the floor amid the toys and built a tower of bricks for Zoe, which she promptly knocked down. Kelly joined him near the toy box. Annabelle fetched toy after toy, giving them to her, until she had a whole heap.

Sean's phone chimed. "Excuse me a moment," he said, pulling it out of his pocket. He checked the display and answered.

He chatted with someone who obviously wanted advice on a change of medication for a patient. As soon as he ended the call, he rose to his feet. "Let me show you to your room so you can settle in."

They went next door to a beautiful bedroom with

light oak furniture and floor and a white bedspread. All clean lines and no fuss. The front wall was made up of glass sliding doors that opened onto a balcony over the river.

"Amazing. I should be paying you to stay here!" Kelly unlatched the doors and stepped out. Despite the chill the view was fantastic. The balcony was edged with frameless glass panels to prevent the babies from falling over.

"You won't say that after a few days with the monsters." Sean lifted Annabelle up and blew on her belly, making her laugh. "Okay, you pong. Time for a diaper change. This is where the extra hands come in useful."

Kelly came back inside and shut the doors. "I'm ready and willing. I'll take Annabelle, since she and I have made friends."

"Good idea." Sean sat Zoe on his hip, then his phone rang again. He sat on the bed and Kelly did the same, pulling Annabelle into a hug. The little girl came into her arms, tucking her head into Kelly's neck. She rocked the baby, her heart swelling with pleasure and contentment. This was her dream come true.

"Hi, Cam," Sean said. "How's Alice?... A false alarm. Oh, well, you won't have long to wait. The baby will arrive by Christmas."

Kelly froze, listening closely.

"Yeah, last night was fun. Thanks... Actually, Kelly is here now... No, she's working for me, looking after the girls."

Cameron had called Sean to ask about last night instead of asking her. Pain twisted in her chest. He had been her best friend, but since he married Alice he'd grown more distant. She and Cameron had been an item once, many years ago. She had set him free, knowing she could never give him children, thinking it was best to get out before their relationship got too serious.

She'd thought it was enough to be his friend and work with him. Too late she realized her stupid heart belonged to him. She had hoped he would never find anyone else and one day they might get together again.

Kelly pressed her face against Annabelle's golden curls and inhaled her sweet baby smell, breathing through the pain of a loss she should have gotten over many years ago. It was time she moved on and left Cameron Knight in the past.

Having a woman in his kitchen again seemed strange. Kelly stood beside Sean, chopping up tomatoes as he washed a lettuce. No woman had been in here since his wife—except Monique, of course, but he thought of the twenty-year-old more as a girl than a woman. She was certainly far too young for him.

"I didn't mean for you to have to look after me as well as the children," he said.

"It's no problem." Kelly flashed him a grin as she scooped up the tomato pieces and dumped them in the salad bowl. "I'm happy to do everything Monique does. I can manage a little cooking and cleaning for a few weeks. It'll be fun looking after your beautiful house."

Did she also think it would be fun looking after him? A flash of awareness spread through Sean and he shoved it away, distracting himself by putting the lasagna in the oven. Kelly was his employee now. That put her out of bounds as surely as if she'd been an army medic. Nothing had changed.

A little voice in the back of his head whispered that maybe he'd made a mistake by employing her. Maybe he should have dated her instead. But he'd been desperate for reliable help with his twins. The girls always came first. Any sort of love life for him was way down the list near the bottom, after his children and his army duties.

Kelly was heading overseas in a few weeks anyway. She was unlikely to be looking for a relationship at the moment. Although Cameron had suggested she might be interested.

Heck, this line of thought was getting him nowhere.

Kelly brushed her hands together and stepped back. "We're about done here until the lasagna is ready." She glanced at the pasta box for cooking instructions.

As she tilted her head, her mass of long reddish hair fell forward, catching the light. Sean dragged his gaze away and tried to think of something to say. Now the twins were in bed, the situation felt too intimate, here alone with her in his house. Thank goodness he'd be at work during the week. Most evenings he had paperwork to occupy him, so he should be able to get through the next few weeks without succumbing to temptation. The secret was to stay occupied and focus on what he was doing rather than who he was with.

"There are still some rooms you haven't seen. Would you like to finish the tour?" he suggested.

"Good idea."

He strode along the ground floor corridor to the end. "This is a wet room meant for when you've been kayaking or boating." He pushed the door open, snapped on the light, and she put her head inside. The kayak paddles rested on hooks on the wall and wetsuits hung on rails. "The kayaks are stored under the house, if you're interested."

"Doesn't look as though you use this room much."

"I used to go out occasionally but I don't have time now." That was the story of his life. About the only thing he managed in the way of exercise was thirty minutes in the gym in the mornings if he woke up early.

"This is a home cinema." He pushed open the next door and turned on the light. A huge screen filled one wall and a couple of rows of comfy chairs faced it. "It's also got a pretty good sound system. I occasionally chill out and listen to music when the girls are in bed. Feel free to come in here whenever you want."

"Do the twins watch kids' programs on the big screen?" Kelly asked.

"Monique brings them here sometimes. I have occasionally, but my time with them is limited, so I prefer to play with them."

Kelly opened the next door and snapped on the light, peering in curiously. The familiar smell of oil paint hit him with a truckload of painful memories. Sean hesitated, his chest tight with emotion, even as he told himself it was just another room. "This was my wife's studio."

"Oh, I'm sorry, Sean. Cameron told me you lost her. I shouldn't have barged in." She stepped back and reached to turn off the light.

"Go ahead. It's fine. Take a look. Monique cleans in here."

Monique did clean in here. That was no lie. But Sean avoided the room. Eleanor had never wanted him inside while she worked and his sense of being unwelcome remained. He was crazy to feel this way. It was just a room. He should clear the space out and use it for something, maybe turn it into a playroom for the girls. After a moment of reluctance, he braced himself and stepped over the threshold.

"Are you sure you don't mind me being in here?" Kelly asked.

For a few seconds, Sean had forgotten she was there. He nodded, not trusting his voice.

Kelly's perceptive gaze lingered on his face, then she turned and surveyed the huge airy space where Eleanor had created her masterpieces.

Kelly wandered across to the stacks of canvases leaning against the wall. "May I take a look?"

He shrugged. She lifted a canvas, then turned it over

21

to see the painting. "Wow. This is amazing. It's so vibrant and colorful. Your wife was very talented."

"Eleanor was fairly well known." He eyed the many canvases, wondering how much they were worth. Quite a lot, he guessed. As always seemed to be the case, her pictures had increased in value after her death. They would be Zoe and Annabelle's inheritance.

When he first met Eleanor, he'd been invigorated and excited by her work, like everyone else. Eventually that changed. If she wasn't there to nag him and shout at him, her damned paintings did it for her. Eleanor's vibrant colors screamed at him from every wall. After her death he had taken them all down and put them in here so he didn't have to look at them.

"Is this a self-portrait?" Kelly moved to stand in front of the only picture Sean had left hanging.

"Yes. I thought the girls should see what their mother looked like."

"She was beautiful. I'm very sorry for your loss." Kelly turned somber brown eyes his way.

"Thank you." Sean averted his gaze, a riot of conflicting emotions charging through him. Part of him wanted to tell her the truth that nobody knew—that he and Eleanor hadn't been happy.

The usual stringent mix of guilt and relief seared his nerves.

"Are you all right, Sean?" Kelly came up behind him and rested a comforting hand on his back.

"Yes, look, I have a paper to write. I'd better get to it. Watch the television if you want." Before he finished speaking, he was already walking away. He ran up the stairs and slipped into the twins' bedroom. Leaning back against the door he blew out a breath, then stepped lightly up beside Zoe's crib. He laid a gentle hand on her head and leaned over the wood-slatted side to kiss her cheek before tiptoeing across the room to Annabelle to do the same.

The moment he had seen his daughters' tiny squashed faces, they'd stolen his heart. It had nearly destroyed him when Eleanor took them away. She knew just how to hurt him. She thrust in the knife and twisted it, threatening to take the girls out of the country so he couldn't see them.

He would rather walk over hot coals than get tangled up in another relationship. The pleasure of female company was simply not worth the pain.

Chapter Three

Kelly jumped out of bed after a restful night's sleep, eager to start her day caring for Zoe and Annabelle. She had a quick shower and dressed in jeans and a sweater, tying her hair back so it didn't get tangled with little fingers before adding a touch of lip gloss and mascara.

The sound of babbling baby voices from the next room made her rush to slip on her shoes. She dashed out of her door, nearly colliding with Sean.

Laughing, he grabbed her shoulders to steady her. "You're in a hurry."

"I heard the twins were awake."

He held up a baby monitor. "Me too. They usually wake up sometime between seven and eight. They're early this morning."

Sean stepped back and she noticed he was wearing shorts and a T-shirt. His arms and legs were all lean, toned muscle, his skin dusted with golden hairs and gleaming with sweat.

"I have a gym above the garage," he said, obviously noticing her appraisal. "I try to get out there at least two mornings a week for a workout. A couple of times a year, the army sends me away for a few weeks of physical training. It's hell if I don't keep my fitness level up."

"Well, you look fit enough to me." Kelly blushed at

his answering grin.

She held his gaze for a moment, tension humming between them. One of the twins squealed, breaking the mood. Sean rubbed the back of his hand over his top lip. "Time to bathe and feed the munchkins. I normally take them in the bath with me, but that's probably not the best idea if you're going to help."

His grin was back, dimples in evidence, eyes sparkling with mischief. Kelly relaxed and smiled, relieved to find him in a good mood this morning. Yesterday evening she'd felt terrible about upsetting him over his wife.

"I don't mind if you don't," she retorted, playing him at his own teasing game.

He chuckled as he pushed open the babies' bedroom door.

"How are my little angels today?"

Both girls chattered at once, some dada sounds clear among the cute noises.

"Hello, Zoe, hello, Belles. I'm going to help Daddy give you a bath this morning." Kelly went to Annabelle first, more sure of her welcome. Her breath rushed out with pleasure as the baby held up her arms, asking Kelly to lift her out of her crib.

"What a big girl you are, Belles." She hugged the child and kissed the top of her head before setting her on the ground.

Her gaze collided with Sean's, the approval in his eyes warming her.

"Annabelle certainly took to you quickly. Let's hope Zoe feels the same way by the end of today. I'll have to leave you alone with them tomorrow and I want you all to be happy together."

"I'm sure we'll be fine. When you're not here, Zoe will turn to me. Remember, I've had lots of experience of dealing with children when I was a pediatric nurse."

"I'm probably just an overprotective dad."

"I'd say you're a normal caring dad. Children of their age often suffer from separation anxiety when left with strangers. It's sensible to be cautious."

Sean picked up Zoe while Kelly held Annabelle's hand as they walked down the hall to the large family bathroom at the end of the corridor. A huge tub sat in the center of the modern room with twin sinks on one wall and a bidet and toilet on another.

As the bath filled with warm water, they undressed the babies, then lifted them in. Kelly and Sean kneeled side by side, playing with the children while they washed them.

The girls squealed with excitement, chattering and splashing. Kelly brushed Annabelle's teeth and soaped her down with a sponge, enjoying the games, as Sean did the same for Zoe.

His T-shirt sleeve stretched tightly on his clenched biceps as he gripped a plastic duck and bobbed it through the water, quacking. Even though her attention was fixed on Annabelle, every cell in her body seemed to realign towards Sean.

He leaned over to kiss Zoe and she pushed his face away.

"Don't you want Daddy to kiss you?" He laughed when Zoe patted his cheeks, babbling so seriously she obviously had something important to say.

"You don't like Daddy's prickly face, do you, angel?"

She shook her head.

He ran a hand around his jaw, a wry smile on his lips. The rasping sound of stubble against his palm sent a tingle through Kelly. She tore her gaze away from his face. She had kissed this man only a few days ago. If she closed her eyes she could remember the sensation, the slight roughness of a day's growth of beard against her skin.

He reached across her to grab a washcloth, the corded muscles in his forearm brushing her hand. The steamy heat clung to her face. For a moment she couldn't catch her breath. She wanted to kiss Sean again, wanted to kiss him properly.

"Time to get out." He lifted Zoe into a big fluffy towel and set her before Kelly. "I'm sure Kelly would like to dry you, angel."

"Oh, yes. I'd love that." The little girl looked over her shoulder at her daddy, but didn't complain as Kelly rubbed her down. "Progress, I believe," Kelly said to Sean.

"Looks like it."

Once both children were dry and dressed, they took them downstairs and sat them in their high chairs for breakfast. Kelly dished out fruit and baby cereal while Sean rushed upstairs for a quick shower.

Fifteen minutes later, he reappeared, shaved, wearing faded jeans and a thick check shirt. "You're all doing fine without me. I don't think you need Daddy."

"Oh, I think we need Daddy," Kelly said.

He eyed her speculatively for a moment before pouring himself a cup of coffee and dropping bread in the toaster.

Later they all wrapped up in coats, scarves, and hats. Sean pushed the twins along the path beside the river in a double stroller, Kelly at his side.

She sucked in a breath of cold air, staring up at the pale blue winter sky through bare tree branches. The river gurgled past, the children chattered, and she and Sean talked about her most recent deployment in Africa, where she'd worked in a field hospital with Cameron.

This was what it must be like to be married with a family—to walk with her husband and children on a Sunday afternoon, an easy, relaxed companionship. A pang of loneliness stole through her. She paused, pretending to examine something on the water while she regained her composure.

27

She was looking forward to her new job nursing for the children's charity. Helping those poor kids would give her huge satisfaction. But this was her dream, having a husband and children of her own.

Something she could never have.

She thought she'd come to terms with the situation a long time ago, but being here with Sean and his girls stripped away her defenses, leaving those bare nerves exposed again.

Maybe she had made a mistake taking this job. Or maybe she should live this dream to the max while she had the chance.

Would it be such a terrible thing to have a fling with Sean? It had been so long since she'd taken any time to enjoy herself. It could never come to anything, of course. His heart obviously still belonged to his beautiful wife and Kelly would be gone in a few weeks. But she had an inkling he might enjoy some female company if there were no strings attached.

Kelly crouched just inside the open front door with a protective arm around each of the two little girls. They blinked sleepily, still in their pajamas, but Kelly had wanted them to see their daddy off to work. It was important they say good-bye to him and understand he would be back at the end of the day.

"You be good girls for Kelly. Daddy will see you at bedtime, okay?" He stooped and kissed each girl on her forehead then straightened, his briefcase in his hand. "Feel free to use the SUV whenever you like," he said. "I've insured it for you to drive."

"That's great, thanks."

He pressed his lips together, obviously reluctant to leave. "You're sure you'll be all right?"

"Certain."

"If you need me, you have my mobile number. I'm not scheduled to operate today, but it's always possible an emergency might come in. If you can't get me, leave a message with my secretary."

"No problem. I know the drill."

"Yes, of course. You're ex-army nursing corps." He tapped his hat against his thigh and breathed out a steamy breath in the cold air. A wood pigeon cooed nearby as the early morning sun streaked fingers of gold across the sky and glinted off Sean's hair.

"Okay, well, see you later then."

He strode towards the sports car, popped the locks, and tossed his briefcase and hat onto the passenger seat, then slid inside.

Kelly was so used to seeing men in uniform, she hardly noticed these days, but she had to admit Sean's broad shoulders and narrow hips filled out his tailored jacket and trousers well. Mind you, he'd probably look good in anything.

The car window lowered and he smiled as he started the engine.

"I thought I might take the twins to see Alice and her son today, if that's okay with you." Kelly raised her voice to be heard over the noise.

"Of course. Give her my regards."

"See you later." She waved as he drove away. "Wave to Daddy," she encouraged the girls. Annabelle did but Zoe hugged Kelly's side and put a thumb in her mouth, her cheek hot and red.

The poor little thing was teething. That probably accounted for how much quieter than Annabelle she was at the moment.

Kelly led them back inside, anticipation bubbling through her as she took them upstairs to have their bath. She was finally alone with the babies, solely responsible for looking after them until Sean came home. Today she'd have a taste of what it was like to be a mum.

Bathed, dressed, and fed, she strapped the girls in

their car seats and stopped at the grocery store for a few things, enjoying wandering around with the twins in the double seats on the front of the shopping cart.

Stocked up, she loaded everything in the SUV before heading for Alice and Cameron's house.

The Edwardian farmhouse lay down a half-mile dirt road amid farmland. Scaffolding covered one wall and a patch of roof was draped with a tarpaulin. Construction workers' vehicles were parked nearby and two men in hard hats carried planks of wood inside.

Alice and Cameron had a lot on their hands with a new home to remodel and a baby on the way. Rain spattered against the windshield as Kelly stopped outside the front. She knocked on the door before she took the girls out of the car, then dashed inside with them one by one, making sure they didn't get wet.

"Hello, Alice. How are you feeling?" They exchanged a brief kiss on the cheek.

"Like a tank." Alice stepped back to let them inside and knocked the hall table. She caught the vase on top before it tumbled off. "I'm so clumsy. I can't move without breaking something." She linked her fingers over her huge belly with a sigh.

"You look beautiful, and you'll only be pregnant for another couple of weeks."

"I don't feel beautiful. I feel fat and ugly."

"I bet Cameron doesn't agree."

"Cameron says what he thinks I want to hear."

Kelly was certain Cameron would never think Alice was ugly. Kelly had been there when he first met Alice in Africa. She was admitted to the field hospital with black eyes, a swollen nose, and a broken arm, waiflike and battered. Even then Cameron had been attracted to her.

Kelly had tried very hard not to be jealous and done her best to help Alice.

"Come to the kitchen and have a cup of tea. That's

the family room at the moment. Everywhere else is a mess."

Banging sounded somewhere close by and an electric drill droned intermittently.

"The work on the house was supposed to be finished by now, but they're nowhere near done."

Annabelle toddled in front of them. Kelly held Zoe's hand as she followed Alice down the hall towards the kitchen. They sat at a stripped pine table while the kettle boiled. With a restored flagstone floor and pine kitchen units topped with a granite counter, this room had obviously been finished.

Alice and Cameron's adopted son, Sami, lay on a rug on the floor, pushing a small car around, creating an engine noise in his throat that only little boys could make.

Kelly crouched and stroked a hand over his hair. "Hello, Sami, love. How are you?"

He grinned up at her. He'd been a poor orphaned baby when she first saw him. It was wonderful to see the happy, healthy eighteen-month-old boy he'd grown into.

Alice grunted as she lowered herself into a chair. "It felt like the contractions had started the night of Sean's birthday, but no such luck." Alice gave Kelly a curious look. "Speaking of Sean, what happened between you two? I thought that kiss might lead to something, and here you are with his children."

"He's employing me for three weeks while his au pair's away."

Alice raised her eyebrows, her blue eyes twinkling. "So you're living with him."

"Not in *that* way."

"Cam and I hoped you two would hit it off. You know Sean's the hospital heartthrob, don't you? Cam says all the nurses are in love with him but he never dates."

Zoe toddled over and tried to climb on Kelly's lap. The baby had well and truly accepted her now. She lifted the little girl and cuddled her close, stroking her hair away from her forehead before laying the back of her hand on Zoe's hot cheek. "She might need something to take down her temperature. It's just a tooth, but it's giving her trouble."

"I can give you some baby pain-relief syrup. It's up there." Alice pointed at a cupboard.

Kelly grabbed the bottle off the shelf and put a teaspoonful in Zoe's mouth.

"So, any chance you and Sean will become more than friends?" Alice asked.

"Anything's possible. Although I think he's still hung up on his wife. That's probably why he won't date. He got very upset the other night when he showed me her studio."

Kelly cuddled Zoe closer, rubbing the baby's back in soothing circles. She shouldn't probe into Sean's personal life, but she was curious. "Do you know anything about his wife?"

"I never met her. Olivia and Radley didn't like her much, though. Radley thought she was selfish. The whole world revolved around her and what she wanted. Sean's career had to take second place."

"Interesting." And not at all what Kelly had expected to hear. "One thing's for sure, she was a beauty."

"Are you surprised?"

Kelly pictured Sean. "I guess not." With Sean's looks, he could have his pick of the most beautiful women. So why didn't he?

The kettle boiled. Kelly made a pot of tea and they chatted about babies and ate cookies, breaking off small pieces to give the children.

"I'd better take these two little darlings back home for some lunch," Kelly said. "If you need me for anything, don't hesitate to call. You have my mobile number."

"Thanks. I might do that. Cam got paged yesterday evening to fly out to pick up some casualties. I'm not sure when he'll be home. I have Radley and Olivia not far away, but it doesn't hurt to have another person to call just in case. I really don't want to give birth in the back of a taxi."

Alice struggled to stand and Kelly rounded the table, offering her an arm. She and Alice embraced and she held her for a few moments. "I'm sure everything will work out fine with the baby. I *am* here if you need me. I'm not a midwife, but I know a lot about pediatrics."

She wanted to reassure Alice. She had always liked her, yet her feelings for Cameron had made her hold back from letting them become good friends. It was long past time she got to know Alice better.

Chapter Four

Sean stripped off his clothes and hung his uniform on a hanger, then pulled on the pants and top of his green scrubs. He pushed his feet into the white plastic clogs he wore in the OR and checked the time. Normally he'd be heading home now. Today he would miss putting his daughters to bed, and having dinner with Kelly.

He enjoyed his quiet evenings alone with Kelly, chatting about army life. From her he'd learned what it was like working as a trauma nurse in a field hospital, giving front line care to battlefield casualties. Plastic surgeons weren't utilized that early in the treatment process. His expertise came in later, so he would never experience overseas deployment. But it sounded like a challenge she'd enjoyed.

His phone rang and his secretary informed him the army Aeromed aircraft under Cameron's command had just landed at Brize Norton. The flight had brought in the seriously injured soldier Sean was preparing for. An ambulance was bringing the man straight to the hospital. That gave Sean about fifteen minutes before he was needed in the OR.

He dialed his home number. Kelly picked up almost immediately and he explained he would be late.

"No problem. Hope the procedure is a success. I'll see you later."

"Don't bother to wait up for me."

"Okay."

With a strange reluctance, Sean cut the connection. He stared at his phone, imagining Kelly in the kitchen, preparing dinner for the girls. Blowing out a breath, he dropped his phone in his locker along with his wallet and other valuables. It was time to clear his mind and focus on the operation ahead.

Sean headed down the hall to the area for scrubbing up, put on his cap and mask, then washed his hands and arms. Radley came in and did the same, then they held out their hands to be gloved and gowned.

A nurse popped her head around the door. "They're bringing the patient in now."

"Thanks."

Sean followed Radley into the restricted area of the surgical suite. The OR was alive with activity as machines bleeped and the medical team prepared the patient.

The man's injured right arm was supported on a special table extension. A nurse cut the dressing away. Sean examined the blast damage, his heart falling. The limb was a mess, the man's lower arm seriously compromised. The injury itself had caused severe trauma, but it looked as though whoever had removed the damaged bone, tissue, and shrapnel in the field hospital had excised too much tissue, creating a larger wound.

"They've made the job of reconstructive surgery almost impossible," Radley said, his voice grim.

"I'd say the viability of the limb is in question," Sean added.

"Let's take it one step at a time." Radley gave some instructions to the team. A nurse fitted his eye loupes on for him and then did the same for Sean so they had a magnified view for the fine surgical procedure.

"I hope none of you had anything planned this

evening," Radley said. "We'll be here awhile."

Sean put his head down and started the slow, careful process of assessment, dictating a plan for reconstruction into a microphone. "I'll take a skin graft from his shoulder for this section." He pointed at the man's forearm.

Radley nodded, concentrating on the tendons to the fingers. That was their pattern, how they worked so well together. Radley did the internal work, repairing bones, ligaments, and tendons, while Sean concentrated on creating a visually acceptable outcome for the patient, often grafting skin, muscle, and bone from other parts of the body to restore the use of a limb.

They worked side by side for hours, exchanging comments and suggestions, their concentration absolute. Sometimes Sean forgot there was anyone else in the room except the patient and Radley. After a long time, they stepped back to assess the situation.

Sean blinked, his eyes bleary. "We've made progress, but I don't know what we're going to do about the hole in the back of his hand."

"There are ligaments and bones missing as well. If we're going to give him a fighting chance of walking away from this with a functioning hand, we'll need to replace them."

"With what?" Sean said.

Radley met Sean's gaze over his mask. "That's the question."

Sean glanced around at the weary team who'd all been working for hours. "We've done what we can for now. Let's call it a day. We'll have a case meeting tomorrow morning and discuss how we'll move forward."

They stepped aside as a nurse moved in to apply a dressing to the arm. The patient had been through a difficult procedure and needed a chance to recover some strength before the next stage.

Sean and Radley walked out. They stripped off their masks, gowns, and gloves, dumped them in the receptacles provided, then headed back towards their rooms together.

"By the way," Radley said, "I meant to ask. How did you get along with the bunny girl?"

"I'm employing her."

Radley's eyebrows rose.

"To look after my twins."

"Ah." Radley chuckled. "Cameron and Alice seemed to think you needed help getting a date."

"Yeah, right." A pretty nurse sashayed towards them, batting her eyelashes in their direction. "When I want a date, I'll choose my own."

Despite his words, he secretly thought Cameron and Alice had done a darn good job by choosing Kelly.

He smiled, thoughts of her drifting through his weary mind like a balm to his soul.

"So, any ideas about the reconstruction of the patient's hand?"

Sean's expression sobered. "I'll review the literature."

"Good idea. We'll talk tomorrow."

They parted company when Sean reached his office door. He stripped and put on his uniform. A splash of cold water on his face would help him stay awake on the way home. Then he headed down to his car.

By the time he tapped in the gate code and stopped in front of River View House, it was nearly midnight. He cut the sports car engine and sat for a moment, pinching the bridge of his nose. There must be a way to repair the man's hand to make it both functional and visually acceptable. If another surgical team had come up against this issue and solved it, he could copy what had been done before. If not, he would have to be creative. Often surgery like this was as much art as science.

He climbed out and fitted his key in the front door lock. As he closed the door behind him, footsteps sounded.

Kelly stood in the kitchen doorway at the end of the hall, the low light shining through her long waves of dark red hair, giving her a shimmering mahogany halo. "Hello. How did the operation go?"

She had waited up for him. A burst of pleasure pushed back the tide of weariness for a moment. "Good as far as it goes. The man will need a number of surgeries before we're finished."

"Don't dwell on it now. It's time to switch off. You should eat and get some sleep."

Sean blinked his gritty eyes. He was pleased to see her, but all he wanted to do was fall into bed. He glanced up the stairs and she moved towards him. "Eat first."

She was all business as she splayed a palm on his back to propel him in the direction of the kitchen. He sat on a stool at the island, the delicious smell of coffee and toast making his mouth water. He hadn't realized how hungry he was.

Kelly poured him a cup of coffee with two sugars and cream, just as he liked it. She pulled a toasted cheese and ham sandwich from under the heat, cut it up, and passed him the plate. "I knew you wouldn't want too much to eat, but you need something."

"Thanks." It was more than Eleanor had ever done for him, or Monique for that matter. She left him a cold sandwich if he was going to be late.

Kelly leaned her elbows on the other side of the island and watched him eat, like a mother making sure her child cleaned his plate.

"I know how it feels to be exhausted after a long operation. It wipes out your appetite, even when you really need to eat," she said. "It got like that during busy periods in the field hospital. After the worst engagements, we were working nonstop for three or four days with barely a moment to eat or drink and certainly no sleep."

"I guess what I do is tame by comparison."

"I've watched surgeons work, the total concentration they need. You must have been in the OR for about four hours. Even with the modern facilities of a high-tech hospital, that's exhausting."

She took his dirty plate and slotted it in the dishwasher. "Okay, Colonel Fabian, sir, time for bed. We don't want you falling asleep in the kitchen."

"It wouldn't be the first time."

"No. I thought not." Kelly stood over him as he dragged himself up from the stool.

How strange it was to have a woman here who understood what he did and how he felt. If he'd married Kelly instead of Eleanor, he'd have been much happier.

Kelly woke to the sound of a baby whimpering. She kept her bedroom door ajar to hear the twins at night. She'd become so attuned to them, even the slightest murmur of distress pulled her from sleep.

She rubbed her eyes and slipped from the bed. Putting on a fleece jacket over her pajamas to ward off the chill, she padded barefoot down the hall to the next bedroom.

Although she hadn't heard him, Sean had beaten her there. Silhouetted by moonlight, he sat on a rocking chair in front of the window with one of his daughters held close, her head resting on his shoulder.

A wave of warm emotions stole through Kelly at the adorable sight of Sean cuddling his baby daughter. He had been wiped out when he arrived home, barely able to keep his eyes open. Although she'd had ample proof he was a hands-on dad, doing everything he could for his daughters while he was here, she hadn't expected him to stir until morning, let alone get out of bed to tend to his child.

A quick glance at the cribs confirmed her suspicion it was Zoe.

"Is it her teeth?" Kelly whispered, not wanting to disturb Annabelle who slept on.

Sean's head came up and he blinked sleepily. "I think so. When did she last have something for the discomfort?"

"Before bedtime, so it's fine to give her another dose."

"Okay. I'll fetch the medicine." He started to get up.

"No. Let me. You stay there."

Kelly went downstairs to retrieve the bottle of pain-relief syrup and a dosing spoon, then hurried back.

Sean rocked slowly in the chair, his cheek against Zoe's hair. He turned his head as Kelly entered and sat straighter, adjusting Zoe so she could take her painkiller.

Kelly crouched beside them and filled the spoon."

Here you are, poppet. This will make you feel better."

The little girl pressed her face into Sean's chest.

"Hey, munchkin, look at Daddy." Sean eased her away and cupped her chin in his hand. "This will stop your tooth hurting. Will you be a good girl and take the medicine for Daddy?"

She nodded. When Kelly offered the spoon again, Zoe opened her mouth and took it without complaint.

As Kelly screwed on the bottle lid, Zoe snuggled deeper into Sean's arms, curling up like a baby animal in a nest, obviously comforted by her father's touch.

Both father and daughter looked adorable with their golden hair mussed and their sleepy faces. Kelly laid an affectionate hand on Sean's arm and smiled at the Superman logo on the front of his pajama top. Whoever had given him that was spot-on. She doubted it was the sort of gift his wife would have thought of, though.

According to Alice, Sean's wife hadn't supported his career. That wasn't uncommon in the army; partners often got fed up with their army spouses being away. But Sean's wife was one of the lucky ones. His medical specialty meant he had always been posted in the UK.

How could any woman not support a husband who spent his time saving the lives of soldiers who protected this country's freedoms and democratic way of life?

If Sean had been her husband, she would have supported him and then some. "Shall I take over so you can get some sleep?"

"No, I've got this. I missed putting the girls to bed. It's good to spend a little time with Zoe now."

"Okay." Kelly rose, reluctantly removing her hand from his arm, and placed the medicine bottle on the changing unit at his side. "It's nearly four, so she can have another dose about breakfast time."

He nodded. There was no reason for her to stay. She should go back to bed, but her feet didn't move. The warm, sleepy atmosphere and the gentle sound of the babies' breathing lulled her. She wanted to curl up in the other chair, to be part of this intimate family moment and watch Sean and Zoe together.

"Can I get you anything, Sean? A drink, maybe."

"Actually, a glass of water would be great. I didn't drink as much as I should yesterday. I'm a little dehydrated."

Pleased to help, she hurried downstairs again and returned with a glass of iced water from the fridge dispenser.

She handed it across and watched him down all of it. He blinked sleepily. Without thought, Kelly placed her hand over his against Zoe's back. She was drawn to touch him, wanted to snuggle up with him and his baby.

His gaze rose to meet hers. For a moment they stared at each other in the moonlight, her whole body alive at the simple contact of his skin against hers.

This man was so much more than a good-looking face, he was kind and gentle. She was already halfway in love with him.

If Sean asked her to stay here, she would change her plans in a heartbeat. She had avoided relationships because she couldn't have children and most men wanted a family. But Sean already had his daughters. Maybe he and his babies were the answer to her prayers, a ready-made family who needed a wife and mother to make them complete.

Chapter Five

Kelly pushed the double stroller between the rows of cut Christmas trees at the garden center and stopped beside Sean. He lifted out a six-foot tree and shook it to spread the branches.

"What about this one?" He grinned at her from beneath his woolly cap decorated in snowmen, a matching scarf wrapped around his neck. He looked as excited as a small boy in a toy shop.

"Looks good to me."

Kelly crouched beside the stroller next to the little girls and pointed at the tree. "What do you two think? Do you like this one?" Both babies stared at her blankly.

"They don't understand what it's for," she said.

"They will when we get it home and cover it in shiny, sparkly things they want to play with."

Zoe yawned and Annabelle grunted, tugging impatiently on the safety straps holding her in the stroller.

"They're bored. Let's buy some decorations quickly and get them home."

Sean passed the tree off to a member of the garden center staff to take to the checkout, then they all traipsed inside the huge glass building full of potted plants and other gardening accessories. They headed to the section overflowing with glittering Christmas baubles, lights, and wreaths. Tall pines dressed in a multitude of colors filled the area to entice shoppers to try the designs.

"Let's go for a traditional look." Sean frowned at a tree decorated with feathers, lace, and old-fashioned pictures of scantily clad women.

"I agree." Kelly hadn't been Christmas tree shopping since she was young. This trip with Sean and the girls was nostalgic, taking her back to a time when her family had lived in England and she'd been close to her parents and sister.

"What do you have at home in the way of Christmas stuff," she asked, thinking they should match the colors.

"Nothing. Eleanor and I never bothered to decorate the house. We were both too busy to give it much thought."

"Same for me. I'm normally working overseas during Christmas." By choice, but she didn't say that aloud.

"This will be my first Christmas with the children." Sean held up a fat Santa-shaped bauble. "I'm really looking forward to it." Then he added softly for her ears only, "I want a happy Christmas to blot out the memory of what happened last December."

Kelly cast him a sympathetic glance and squeezed his arm. Last Christmas was around the time his wife died. That must be a terrible holiday memory. She was surprised he could bring himself to celebrate at all.

Sean lifted a wreath of holly and pine twined with shiny gold and red beads. "This will look good over the wood-burning stove in the sitting room area."

They filled a cart with garlands, baubles, and other fripperies, checked out, and loaded everything in the car. Both girls fidgeted and moaned, tired and fretful now, ready for lunch and a nap.

Sean fixed the tree to the roof of his SUV with the help of the garden center assistant. The pine blew and bumped on top of the vehicle as Sean drove home, its fluttering branches visible through the glass sunroof. Annabelle cried and pointed at it, while Zoe screamed in distress.

An earsplitting noise filled the car, so loud Kelly couldn't make herself heard as she tried to reassure the babies.

"Thank goodness we're only going two miles," Sean shouted, wincing.

When they arrived home, they rushed the girls inside to comfort them, stripping off their thick winter suits, hats, and gloves, changing diapers, wiping noses, and dispensing kisses and hugs until peace was restored.

Once the children were in their high chairs, Kelly hummed a Christmas carol she remembered from childhood as she heated the twins' lunch and prepared soup with warm crusty rolls for herself and Sean.

"You seem happy here, Kelly," Sean said.

"Yes, very happy. I love looking after the girls. And you."

As she sat across the table from him, he reached over and laid his hand on hers, his eyes sparkling with pleasure. "I enjoy having you here. You know that, don't you?"

"I hoped so."

He stroked his thumb across the back of her hand, his expression thoughtful. Was he about to ask her to stay on, or reveal he had feelings for her?

With a sigh, he let her go and resumed eating. Kelly's breath rushed out in disappointment. Maybe he was just grateful to her for stepping in to help with his children. His mind must be on the anniversary of losing his wife—not on starting a new relationship.

After lunch, Sean fixed the tree on its stand and

45

strung the miniature lights around it. Kelly helped Zoe hang the baubles on the branches while Sean assisted Annabelle, both of them lifting the babies so they could reach the higher branches.

It took five minutes for the children to lose interest. They toddled to the sofa, climbed up, and curled together, their thumbs in their mouths. Then they drifted off to sleep, leaving Sean and Kelly to finish decorating the tree.

Kelly grabbed her phone to take some photographs of the two cute little girls cuddling up, her heart aching at the thought that in a few weeks she would probably be many miles away. They would return to their normal routine with Monique and these photos might be all Kelly had to remind her of this wonderful time with the children.

While Sean was busy packing up the wrappings from the decorations, Kelly surreptitiously snapped some shots of him as well—something to dream over when she had a quiet moment.

As the babies slept, Sean dropped onto the sofa beside them and opened a book on his lap, sketching diagrams and making notations.

Kelly slipped her phone back in her bag with a sigh. The last few days he had been preoccupied with important medical problems while here she was mooning over him like a love-sick schoolgirl.

"Thinking about your latest patient?"

He nodded. He'd explained the conundrum of the surgical reconstruction he needed to do. For the last two nights he had pored over his laptop, reading papers and reports of similar operations, studying plans of the musculature of the human body, looking for inspiration.

Kelly brought him a cup of coffee and sat at his side, examining his diagrams. "What about taking muscle from the ribs?"

"Yes." He pointed at his sketch. "I've already discussed that possibility with Radley. The main problem is we need some bones to reconstruct the supporting architecture of the hand before we can graft on the soft tissue.

"Ribs?" Kelly said, her eyebrows raised in question.

"Yes." Sean turned a thoughtful gaze her way. "That's exactly what I'm contemplating. The ribs are the right size and the patient won't miss a couple of them. As far as I can see, it's the only option, but it's never been done before. We'd be pushing the boundaries."

"That's what boundaries are for." Kelly's voice came out husky and intimate. Sitting so close to Sean, their shoulders and thighs touching, she wanted to snuggle into his arms and kiss him. She wanted to be with this man. If she didn't make the first move, she would never know if he felt the same way.

"I want to push some boundaries with you," she said softly.

Sean set aside his pad and turned to her, his hand lifting to cup her cheek. She leaned into his touch, everything inside her melting.

"Kelly," he whispered.

A log crackled in the wood-burning stove and the soft sound of the babies' breathing filled the silence.

They both moved at once, arms sliding around each other, drawing close. He smelled of the outdoors, of crisp winter air and pine trees.

"I keep thinking about my birthday kiss," he whispered. "How it was over too soon."

"Maybe we can have a Christmas kiss," she said. "If we start practicing now, we should be really good at it by Christmas Day."

He chuckled, then his lips covered hers in the endless dreamy kiss she had longed for ever since she met him.

***

With the children in bed and the house silent, Kelly carried two mugs of hot chocolate out onto the deck. She and Sean snuggled together on one of the recliners, wrapped in a fleecy blanket. They stared at the speckled vista of a trillion stars, shining like diamonds strewn across the deepest navy velvet.

"So beautiful," she whispered, hardly daring to speak for fear of breaking this magical moment.

"Yes, you are." Sean pulled her closer and kissed her. She rested her head on his chest and listened to the steady beat of his heart as she sipped her chocolate, trying not to think of the future, content to enjoy this moment.

Earlier, sitting on the sofa in front of the log fire, she and Sean had kissed until the children woke. He had been a gentleman, not rushed her into anything more.

Although she told herself she was heading down a slippery slope towards heartbreak when she had to leave, just this once she wanted some fun without worrying about the future.

Deep inside she acknowledged she wanted more, but after one afternoon of kissing she could hardly ask Sean where he saw their relationship going.

If he just wanted a fling for a few weeks, she was okay with that, but if he wanted more, she would be ecstatic. She would relax and let things develop naturally, secretly hoping he wanted her to stay on. If he did, she could always work for the children's charity in London instead of going overseas.

Maybe, just maybe, she would get to live the life she had always wanted with a husband and children. Maybe this Christmas really would be magical and all her dreams would come true.

Sean hummed as he stepped out of the elevator and strode along the corridor towards the trauma ward.

Thoughts of Kelly hovered in the back of his mind all the time, leaving him tingly and warm. Those he passed must think he was crazy because he kept smiling for no apparent reason.

All his fears of mixing business with pleasure were gone. Kelly would not let anything that happened between them affect how she cared for Zoe and Annabelle, not that he expected any problems between him and Kelly. He'd never met a more sympathetic and understanding woman. He was halfway in love with her and he'd only known her a couple of weeks.

"Good morning, sir," a nurse said as he entered the ward.

He acknowledged her with a nod and opened the door to Pvt. Ewan Tyler's room. His romantic thoughts faded as he assumed a professional demeanor. Sorrow tugged deep in his chest at the sight of the eighteen-year-old lying in the bed, his face a splotchy mass of healing cuts and bruises, his right arm covered in a pressure dressing, the arm Sean and Radley had operated on the previous week.

Private Tyler was little more than a kid, only a few months out of school and into his first tour of duty overseas. Now he was a casualty. More than anything, Sean wanted to give this young man a usable hand back again.

Sean's whole attitude towards the young service men and women who passed through his care had changed since he had kids of his own. Now he could identify totally with the parents he saw sitting white-faced with shock at their youngster's bedside.

Tyler lay awake, an iPod on his pillow, earbuds in his ears. He pulled them out with his good hand and fumbled to switch off the device as Sean approached.

"No hurry, Private. Take your time."

"Yes, sir."

"How are you feeling?"

"Well as can be expected, sir."

The young man had made incredible progress in such a short time. Often soldiers with severe blast injuries suffered from fungal infections due to contamination and the conditions they lived under, but Tyler had tested negative and his face was already healing well.

"Today's the day then, Tyler. You understand what's going to happen?"

"Yes, sir. You're going to take muscle and bone from my ribs to build me a new hand."

Sean nodded, with a smile to encourage the lad. "That's right. It will take a good few months to heal, but with patience and physiotherapy, you should be able to use your right hand for most tasks."

"As long as I can hold my girlfriend's hand, that'll be excellent, sir. She doesn't like holding my left hand. Says I don't hold her right."

Sean smiled, his chest tight with emotion. He didn't usually get this involved with his patients. His feelings for Kelly had stirred him up inside and made him more sensitive.

"Tell your girlfriend she'll have to make do with your left hand for a few months, then she can have the right hand back."

"Yes, sir. Thank you, sir. I appreciate what you're doing for me, Doctor. Mum said this operation is something special."

"We're going to record it as a teaching aid for other surgeons. We'll also have some visiting doctors in the viewing gallery during the operation."

"I'll be the star of the show and sleep through it all," Tyler quipped. The boy was incredibly brave and cheerful considering what had happened to him.

"You certainly are a star, Tyler. You and all our lads who risk their lives."

The young man's expression sobered. "Thank you,

sir. I appreciate your saying so."

"A nurse will be along shortly to prepare you. I'll see you tomorrow to talk you through how things went. Okay?"

"Yes, sir."

Sean nodded and left the ward, heading back to his room to change. Anticipation surged along his veins. He and Radley had planned meticulously. Everything was in place. But there was no escaping the fact this was a radical procedure, something untried and experimental. He prayed it worked and that by next summer Private Tyler could hold his girlfriend's hand.

Chapter Six

Kelly didn't like to leave Zoe and Annabelle in the hospital day care, but it was only for a couple of hours. She really wanted to watch Sean operate. He'd bounced ideas off her before he discussed them with Radley, so she knew exactly how he planned to reconstruct the patient's hand. He'd invited her to join the visiting surgeons in the viewing gallery to watch the idea put into action.

In the day care, two smiling young nursery nurses took the babies' hands. "Hello, Zoe. We haven't seen you for a long time, have we. Come along, Belles, are you going to play with the others?"

With only a moment's hesitation, Zoe toddled off beside the young women. Annabelle didn't even spare Kelly a glance. She trotted away chattering to herself and laid claim to a plastic rocking horse.

"I can see they're going to be fine here," Kelly said to the supervisor.

"Yes, they fit in well. We don't have many tantrums from Colonel Fab's little girls." The woman grinned at the mention of Sean's nickname. Kelly suppressed an eye roll. She supposed she would have to get used to women's reaction to Sean.

After checking the time on her phone, she headed across the car park to the impressive space-age structure of the military hospital. Weak winter sun reflected off the many windows, making the ultramodern building glow.

The main doors swished open as she approached. She crossed the foyer, climbed in the elevator, and selected the restricted access floor where the operating rooms and the senior officers' suites were located. At the beep, she scanned the security pass Sean had given her.

When the elevator stopped, she stepped out and glanced around. She had never worked in the Brize Norton hospital, spending most of her time overseas. This place was state-of-the-art, dedicated to military medicine and staffed completely by joint forces personnel. She felt immediately at home surrounded by uniforms. How would she cope working as a civilian? The reality of leaving the army hadn't sunk in yet. At the moment she still felt like she was on leave, and technically she was.

She followed the signs to the viewing gallery for the theater where Sean and Radley would operate. Although she was early, the rows of tiered seating in the glass enclosure were already filling up with visiting surgeons and medical students. Kelly went down the steps and found the two empty seats at the end of the front row.

Pieces of paper reading RESERVED BY COLONEL FABIAN were stuck on with tape. She sat on one, aware of a few interested glances aimed her way. She avoided the looks and stared down at the large high-tech OR where Sean would be working.

Already the scrub nurses and the medical technicians who monitored the equipment were there preparing.

A few minutes later, someone sat in the other reserved seat. "Hello," Daniel Fabian said with a grin. "Remember me?"

"Yes." She could hardly forget him—the man who had flirted with her the night of Sean's birthday party, despite the fact he had a girlfriend on his arm. She'd felt sorry for the poor woman.

Daniel looked like a slightly tarnished version of Sean with dark blond hair and grayish-blue eyes. He probably had no trouble finding girlfriends to fuel his reputation as a womanizer.

"You're the bunny girl. I'm glad you and Sean got together. You'll be good for him."

"Thanks." She didn't know what Sean had told his brother, so she decided not to say much.

Daniel leaned forward to gaze around the OR. "Wow. Impressive. I thought you army medics operated in bombed-out buildings with equipment held together by string and rubber bands."

Kelly swallowed her laugh. To be honest, he wasn't far wrong. She'd worked in terrible conditions overseas.

"Not in the UK," she said with raised eyebrows.

"Obviously not."

"Sean says you're a plastic surgeon as well." Sean had mentioned his brother a few times with obvious affection.

"Yep. But I don't get to do anything nearly this interesting. At the moment I'm selling my soul for filthy lucre." Daniel glanced over his shoulder and lowered his voice. "I do nose jobs and breast implants for women who have more money than sense. I'm thinking of spreading my wings and following in my big brother's footsteps."

"Spreading your wings, as in joining the army?"

He nodded.

"Wow. That will be a change of pace for you." And a large drop in salary. According to Sean, Daniel was in partnership with their father in an exclusive London clinic. That's where Sean had started out before he joined the army. When he left, it had caused a family rift.

"I can recommend military medicine," she said with honesty. She'd thoroughly enjoyed her time in the army.

The soft murmur of conversation in the viewing gallery quieted as the patient was wheeled into the OR below, and transferred to the operating table. The rest of the medical team followed. She recognized Sean immediately from his tall, lean build, and his air of authority.

Her heart raced and then stalled at the sight of him in his green gown, masked, and gloved with magnifying eye loupes on. What a crazy stupid heart she had being turned on by that! It just proved she was a nurse to the core.

Sean glanced up and met her gaze. A grin tugged at her lips. Even with his face half covered, she could tell he smiled back. Her heart did a little dance and she raised a hand to wave, not caring if everyone thought she was another stupid female besotted with Colonel Fab. She was.

Both Radley and Sean wore microphones. Their easy banter made it clear they were good friends and comfortable working together. They started the operation, narrating the steps of the procedure, explaining their thoughts and actions while cameras filmed from three angles, projecting the images on screens in the gallery.

Silence fell as everyone watched, totally absorbed by what was going on below. Daniel leaned forward, his chin in his hand, eyes fixed on his brother.

Everything proceeded the way Sean had described to her with only a couple of hiccups. Kelly wanted to stay for the whole procedure, but after two hours, it was time to get the girls from the day care. She reluctantly stood and tried to squeeze past Daniel. He rose and headed out as well.

"You didn't need to come with me," she said when they reached the corridor.

He pulled out his phone and checked the screen. "Actually, I did. I have a flight to New York this evening. My phone vibrated a few minutes ago to alert me it was time to leave. I'll walk you out."

They headed to the elevator and climbed in. "So, what did you think?" Kelly asked.

Daniel nodded slowly. "I wish I could stay until the end. That's just the sort of work I should be involved in, using my skills to make a real difference. I feel like I'm coasting right now, not sure which direction to go. But I need to do something meaningful. I can't keep doing what I'm doing for the rest of my life or I'll go crazy."

"So you've decided to join the army?"

"Probably. I want to talk to Sean about it first. My father will go ballistic if I leave the London practice, but I can't live my life to please him. Sean was strong enough to make the break and follow his heart. I must as well."

The elevator's polite computerized voice announced the main floor. They stepped off and headed across the marble and stainless steel foyer to the exit.

"So, are you and Sean a hot item, then?" Daniel cast her a mischievous smile.

"I guess."

"You don't sound certain." A hint of disapproval crept into his voice. "Sean's been hurt badly. Don't mess with him."

"I'm not planning on doing that." If anyone ended up hurt, she was pretty sure it would be her. "The thing is, I'm not certain Sean's ready for a long-term relationship. Isn't he still in love with his wife?"

Daniel laughed without humor, the sudden harsh sound surprising her. "You need to ask him about Eleanor."

Kelly stared at him, wishing he would elaborate.

"Seriously. Ask him," he said, stopping beside a very expensive sports car with the license plate FAB **1.**

He obviously wasn't going to tell her about Eleanor. With a sigh, she admired the car.

"Very nice. Almost worth the price of your soul."

He chuckled. "I used to think so."

"Good luck with your career-changing decision," she said. "I really do recommend the army. I loved it and so does Sean."

With a burst of anticipation, she hurried across the car park to pick up the babies. Tomorrow was Christmas Eve. She couldn't wait to see the girls' cute little faces when they visited Santa Claus in the afternoon. Taking her children to see Santa was a fantasy of hers. Zoe and Annabelle might not be hers, but she was starting to love them as much as if they were.

Kelly leaned into Zoe's crib and tucked the little girl up, kissing her forehead. "Night night, sweetie. Sleep tight." As she crossed to Annabelle's crib for a final kiss, she heard the front door open downstairs.

"I hear your daddy."

So did Annabelle. She sat up, gripping the wooden bars of her crib, and shook the side. "Dada," she shouted.

"Hang on, poppet. I'll go and fetch him."

Buzzing with anticipation, Kelly headed for the top of the stairs.

Sean sat on the hall chair, pulling off his shoes. He stood, hung his hat in the cupboard, and ran his fingers back through his golden hair. She longed to charge downstairs and throw herself into his arms, but she didn't know how he'd feel after a big operation. Over the years, she had worked with many surgeons. Often they needed alone time to recover after a long and difficult procedure.

"Hello. You're just in time to say goodnight to your two little angels," Kelly said.

He glanced up, a smile on his face. "Wonderful. I hoped I'd make it home before they went to sleep."

"How did the op go? I had to leave halfway through, I'm afraid."

"As planned. It was a gamble, but it paid off. I'm relieved for the young patient."

"You're a brilliant surgeon." Kelly grinned down at him.

"Thank you. But I can't take all the credit."

He trod up the stairs in his socks, unbuttoning his jacket. "The whole team planned meticulously. Success is down to teamwork and good preparation."

"Which takes great leadership. As I said, you're a brilliant surgeon."

He wrapped her in his arms and she slid her hands inside his jacket to massage the tight muscles in his back. He kissed her and leaned his forehead against hers. "I am *so* tired. All the research and planning has taken its toll. I feel as though I could sleep for a week."

She tried to step back but he held on to her. Small lines formed between his eyebrows. "Did I say something wrong?"

"Of course not. I just don't want to crowd you. It sounds as though you need some space."

He laughed a low, amused chuckle that rolled across her senses. "Kelly, love, you *are* my space, you and the girls and this house. Just crossing the threshold helps me relax. I've always loved coming back to this house and the twins. Since you arrived, I can't wait to get home. The moment I leave in the morning, I start looking forward to seeing you again."

Kelly snuggled closer to his chest and pressed some kisses to his neck and jaw. He really was an easy man to live with.

"That's better," he whispered. "Now, let's say good night to my two angels."

He held Kelly's hand as he headed to the babies' bedroom, only releasing her to lean over Annabelle's crib and pick up the wide-awake baby.

"Aren't you sleepy, young lady?"

"Dada, Dada," Annabelle kept repeating.

"Daddy is very pleased to see both his beautiful girls." He smiled at Zoe, then kissed Annabelle's cheeks, making her giggle before he deposited her back in her bed. "Time to sleep now, munchkin."

He crossed the room to Zoe, caressing her cheek before leaning down to kiss her. She lay cuddling her teddy, her thumb in her mouth. "How are your teeth, angel? Are they better?"

"I think so," Kelly said. "Her temperature's returned to normal. I wouldn't have left her in the day care if she'd been fussy."

"Good night, angel. Sleep tight." Sean stroked the blonde curls back off Zoe's forehead, gave Annabelle another kiss, then put his arm around Kelly and led her from the room.

"I'll go and check dinner while you change," she said.

"Okay." He kissed her again, releasing her reluctantly. With a thoughtful glance over his shoulder, he headed to his bedroom.

Kelly went downstairs, checked the peanut chicken she had put in the slow cooker earlier, and set some water to boil for the rice.

Sean wandered in wearing faded jeans and a polo shirt, and sat on a stool at the kitchen island. Kelly poured two glasses of wine, setting one in front of him.

"Thanks." He took a sip. "So, you sat beside my disreputable brother today. Did he flirt with you?"

She grinned. "I know you said he has a reputation with the ladies, but I like him."

"So do I. We've always been close. He's my best friend as well as my brother."

Kelly tipped the rice in the boiling water and placed a lid over the pan, then turned, her arms wrapped around her middle. Speaking of Daniel reminded her of what he'd said about Eleanor. She didn't want to upset Sean, but she had to raise the touchy subject.

"He mentioned your wife."

Sean twirled the stem of his wineglass between his fingers on the granite countertop. "What did he say?"

"That I should ask you about her."

He nodded. "Okay."

Kelly waited while Sean took another sip of wine. The fire crackled and the lights on the Christmas tree sparkled, reflecting off the dark windows.

Her instinct was to speak, to fill the awkward silence. Instead she held her tongue, giving Sean time to think.

He glanced up thoughtfully. "The only person I've told the full story to is Dan. Until now." He dragged in a breath and blew it out. "The truth is, Eleanor walked out on me before she died."

"Oh!" Kelly pressed a hand over her mouth. So what she'd heard was right; Sean and Eleanor hadn't been happy together.

"Two weeks after the girls were born, she announced she was leaving me for a wealthy Swiss guy who'd bought some of her paintings. I think she'd been seeing him for a while. I'm not sure. To be honest, all I could think about was losing the twins."

"Oh, Sean, that must have been awful." An inane thing to say, but she couldn't summon anything better with her mind racing to take this in.

"The worst few weeks of my life." He knocked back the rest of his wine and refilled his glass from the bottle. "I had my lawyer working overtime trying to stop her taking the girls out of the country. I was frantic. Then her boyfriend called me. Eleanor had been hit by a taxi outside their hotel and pronounced dead at the scene. He wanted me to come and get the babies.

"I was at work. I walked out of the hospital in a daze, still wearing my scrubs, and drove to central London. Both the girls were hungry and had dirty diapers. The guy wouldn't even touch them. I was numb after hearing about Eleanor, but so unbelievably happy to have my children back."

Kelly's heart pounded in distress imagining how upset Sean must have been at the prospect of losing the two babies he obviously doted on. "Eleanor was going to take them to Switzerland?"

"Yes."

"So you wouldn't have been able to see them."

Sean shrugged. "She told me I was welcome to visit them in Switzerland."

"Why did you keep it a secret that she left you?"

"I was desperately relieved she couldn't take the girls away." He scrubbed a hand over his face and screwed up his eyes. "I felt so bad, so guilty for being pleased to get them back that way."

Rounding the island, Kelly wrapped him in her arms. He turned into her embrace, resting his forehead on her shoulder. She stroked back the sleek golden strands of his hair, willing him to gain comfort from her love and compassion.

"It wasn't your fault she died." Despite her words, Kelly could understand his feelings. What a horrible situation to be in.

"I swore I would never marry again. I won't ever give a woman that sort of power over me and the girls."

Disappointment flashed into Kelly and gripped her heart. She'd been right. He wasn't ready for a relationship. Although she could hardly blame him after what he'd been through.

He lifted his head and ran a thumb across her cheek, staring into her eyes. "You've made me reassess. I like having you here, Kell. I like coming home to you, but I want to take things slowly."

"That's okay with me." Kelly's heart raced, her fingers tracing the soft hair on his nape. She'd keep Sean and his little girls in her life any way she could.

"I'd like to start by dating, but I know you're planning to work overseas. Perhaps we can stay in contact and see each other when you're in this country?"

Kelly's emotions swung all over the place. Despite his earlier comment that he liked coming home to her, he obviously didn't want her living here.

"Why don't I ask the charity if I can work in the UK?"

"You'd do that for me?"

"Of course. I'd love to see you and the girls regularly."

"That sounds great. When Monique comes back we'll be able to spend more evenings out, just the two of us."

The idea of Monique moving back here with Sean grated on Kelly. In the two short weeks she had been here, Sean and his girls had become hers. Given a chance, she would rather stay here and care for them than do any other job. But she could hardly say that. Anyway, it would be mean to steal Monique's position.

"So, when do we start dating?" They had sort of started already with all the kissing they'd done, although that was as far as they'd gone.

"Tomorrow." Sean rose and kissed her. "I'll go in to see Private Tyler in the morning, then I'm on leave until the New Year. We'll take the girls to visit Santa in the afternoon, then you and I have been invited out to dinner in the evening."

The tight knot of concern in Kelly loosened. Sean

was bruised and wary, but he wasn't still in love with Eleanor and he wanted to move on. There was hope that sometime in the future she might be a proper part of this family.

She would have to take good care of him and give him lots of love to restore his trust in women.

Chapter Seven

Chattering adults and laughing children lined up outside the snow-dusted timber chalet at the entrance to Santa's grotto on the fourth floor of the busy London department store.

"We might as well carry the girls through so they're high enough to see everything," Sean said.

"Good idea. Also, they're less likely to be frightened by something if they're in our arms." Kelly followed Sean as he pushed the stroller into the parking area set aside for baby carriers and applied the brake. She lifted Annabelle from her seat while he picked up Zoe.

Kelly hitched her bag higher on her shoulder and handed their booking form to the small woman dressed as an elf in a red hat trimmed with bells.

"Follow the signs to Santa Claus's workshop." The elf lady grinned at the children. "Have fun!"

They pushed through a turnstile, ducked beneath strips of hanging greenery, and entered a dimly lit cave. Tiny mechanical elves lined up at a bench hammered at wooden dolls and trains in time to cheery Christmas music.

Annabelle clutched Kelly's coat collar, wide-eyed with fascination. She pointed at the tableau. "Me, me, me, me," she chanted in her latest refrain. It was her new favorite word and she knew exactly what it meant.

"You can't have those toys," Kelly said. "Santa's elves are still making them. When we reach Santa, he'll give you a present to take home."

Annabelle stared at Kelly, obviously trying to understand. Then she stretched towards the scene again, chattering to herself.

Kelly squinted in the low light, her eyes still not adjusted. "Is Zoe all right?" she asked Sean. As usual, Zoe was the quieter of the two children, cuddled in her daddy's arms, sucking her thumb.

"You're okay, angel, aren't you? You like the elves." Sean dropped a kiss on top of Zoe's hair.

He leaned close to Kelly, pressed his lips to Annabelle's head, and stole a quick kiss from Kelly as well.

"Zoe'll be fine. I might not sit her on Santa's knee, though. I'm willing to bet she won't like that."

They wandered along the winding woodchip path through Rudolph's stable where a huge reindeer model with a flashing red nose nodded its head, past Santa's sleigh piled high with brightly wrapped boxes tied with ribbons, and on to Santa's workshop itself.

Other family groups of mum, dad, and children strolled with them, laughing and enjoying themselves. With a rush of affection, Kelly stroked back Annabelle's hair and held her close. How she loved this sweet little girl and her sister. Anyone seeing their group probably thought she was the twins' mother, and Sean's wife. If only that were true.

Longing swept through her, leaving goose bumps on her skin. She was certainly something to them, but would never be a mother and wife if Sean adhered to what he'd said. He'd been adamant he didn't want to marry again.

She joined in with the Christmas song, singing softly to Annabelle as they passed a traditional festive scene of a decorated tree beside a fireplace with four stockings hung on the mantelpiece, two large ones and two small ones.

Kelly had thought of hanging stockings at Sean's house but in the end she hadn't, feeling awkward about putting one up for herself with the other three. It seemed a bit presumptuous somehow.

An elf ushered them towards a rustic wooden door and Sean pushed it open. "Oh, look, girls. Who can you see?" He held Zoe up and pointed. "There's Santa."

A fat old man in a Santa suit complete with long white beard sat on a wooden stool in a mock log cabin surrounded by sacks of brightly wrapped gifts. "Ho, ho, ho, who do we have here?" he said in a deep voice.

Zoe burst into tears and clung to Sean, burying her face against his chest. Annabelle curled her chubby fingers around Kelly's collar and held on tightly, but she stared at Santa with rapt attention.

"Hello, Santa," Sean said. "We've brought Zoe and Annabelle to see you."

"Have you been good girls this year?" Santa asked.

"Of course they have." Kelly grinned at Annabelle and Zoe, trying to put them at ease. "They're always good girls, aren't you?"

"Do you want to sit on Santa's knee?" the man asked Annabelle.

Kelly had mixed feelings about handing the toddler over to a strange man. Annabelle allowed herself to be carried closer without complaining, but hung on to Kelly for dear life when Santa patted his lap.

"Both the girls are slightly shy," Kelly said with an apologetic smile.

Undaunted, Santa jangled a rod covered in bells. Two old men dressed as elves came in and did a funny little dance. The whole thing was so surreal, Kelly had to swallow back a laugh as her gaze collided with Sean's disbelieving look.

Santa handed a gift to Annabelle and one to Sean for

Zoe. Then the elves hustled them out, presumably making way for the next in line.

They emerged onto a busy aisle in the toy section of the department store.

"Poor baby," Kelly said to Zoe, hoping to distract her by helping her unwrap her present. Zoe stopped crying and grasped the small blue teddy inside, turning it over and trying to pull off its ears. One immediately came loose.

"I think she wants to dissect it," Sean quipped.

"That must be her surgeon genes. You'd better watch out when she's big enough to use a knife."

Sean chuckled. They huddled together as people bustled past in the busy aisle while both girls examined their identical teddies. After a few minutes, Annabelle tossed hers on the floor and pointed at a display of dolls, chanting, "Me, me, me."

Crouching to pick up the discarded toy, Sean tucked it in the front of Annabelle's coat. "Nothing more for you until Christmas Day, Little Miss Fickle. Let's hope that tomorrow Santa can come up with something interesting enough to hold your attention."

"Does Santa have something interesting lined up for tomorrow?" Kelly asked with a grin.

"I hope so. Santa has certainly spent plenty of money on the presents."

Kelly emerged from her bedroom in the only decent dress she owned, a slinky scarlet wraparound. It was shorter than she remembered, falling to mid-thigh level. She'd bought it for a summer vacation in Greece a few years back and it was not really warm enough for winter. She hoped the heating in the restaurant where they ate would be good or she'd have to keep her coat on.

The doorbell chimed. She hurried downstairs to let in Lisa, the teenager from the village who was babysitting for the evening. The sixteen-year-old's eyelashes were caked with mascara, her eyes outlined in black, her lids blue and pink, her lips scarlet. She tottered in on high heels wearing a skirt that barely covered her backside.

Both Kelly and Lisa stared as Sean came down the stairs. Kelly's heart fluttered like a moth trying to get to a flame. For a moment she couldn't catch her breath. She was so used to being around Sean that she forgot how gorgeous he was until she suddenly saw him wearing something different. Tonight was the first time she'd seen him in a suit.

The navy jacket hugged his broad shoulders, the white shirt bringing out the blue of his eyes. He reached for his coat and draped the snowman scarf around his neck, making her smile.

"Hello, Mr. Fab." The teen giggled, striking a pose and pushing out her chest.

"The girls are both asleep," Sean said, giving no indication he even noticed Lisa's flirting. "If they wake, don't go in to them unless they sound distressed. Often they will just go back to sleep. It might unsettle them if they know Kelly and I aren't here. Don't worry about changing diapers; we'll do that when we get home. We won't be late."

"Yes, Mr. Fab. I'll call you if there are any problems." The girl fluttered her eyelashes. "Can I have your mobile number?"

Kelly had to swallow her laugh. Cheeky little minx. "You can have mine," Kelly said, jotting it on the pad by the house phone and handing it over. "Text me if you have any questions while we're out."

The doorbell chimed again, heralding the taxi driver.

"Don't hesitate to call Kelly if necessary," Sean said to the girl as he helped Kelly on with her coat. "We're only going a few miles away, so we can return quickly if the children need us."

68

They climbed in the back of the taxi and Kelly breathed a sigh of relief to be out of the house. It had been hectic spending the afternoon in London at the department store visiting Santa, then driving home in time to go out for dinner.

As she sat in the warm car, the radio playing softly in the background, the reality sank in. This was the first time she and Sean had gone out without the girls. She'd have liked it to be just the two of them, but they were meeting Cameron and Alice, and Radley and his wife, Olivia.

Sean lifted her hand and dropped a kiss on her knuckles. "This is our first real date."

"I was just thinking the same thing."

"I hope it's the first of many." He slid his arm around her shoulders and pressed his lips to her temple. She turned, clutching his lapels, and kissed him properly.

"I didn't get a chance to say how lovely you look," he said. "It's the first time I've seen you in anything but trousers."

"Except for the bunny girl outfit," she reminded him.

"Yep. Except for that." He grinned. "I hope I might see you dressed that way again sometime."

Kelly raised her eyebrows. He'd been very much the gentleman so far. Could he be thinking of taking things further now they were officially dating?

"I'm sure that can be arranged."

He tapped the end of her nose playfully.

A few minutes later, the taxi stopped in front of a row of thatched cottages that had been joined into one building and converted into a restaurant by a local celebrity chef. Sean jumped out and offered her his hand as she negotiated the rough ground in the semidarkness. She rarely wore high heels; they took some getting used to.

Sean opened the low arched door. "Mind your head. I think they were all tiny in the 1500s when this place was built." He ushered her in first and they both ducked under a thick black beam. A huge log fire crackled in the inglenook fireplace flanked by pillars hung with Christmas garlands of holly decorated with tiny gold bells.

Christmas centerpieces graced the many tables and the murmur of conversation filled the candlelit room.

"There they are." Sean put his arm around Kelly's shoulders and led her to the bar area.

"Hello," Cameron said with his usual smile, embracing her.

She waited for the familiar tingle of awareness as Cameron moved close and pressed his cheek to hers. It was still there, but only just. Nothing like the shivery pleasure she felt every time Sean kissed her or touched her.

Cameron turned his attention to Sean. "I gather after the big op that you and Radley are now movie stars."

"Yes, absolutely," Sean said. "We'll be famous among medical students everywhere."

They all chuckled.

The men shook hands and Radley kissed Kelly's cheek.

Kelly moved to Alice's side so they could embrace around her huge belly. "How are you?

Alice fanned herself with a menu, her cheeks bright red. "Roasting. It's like a furnace in here."

"You have a little heater inside you, that's why," Cameron quipped.

She batted him on the arm with the menu. "Don't joke about it. I'm uncomfortable." Despite her words, she smiled at him affectionately.

Sean introduced Kelly to Radley's wife and they greeted each other. Olivia Knight was exactly the sort of woman to suit Radley—tall, slender, and beautiful with an air of quiet competence about her. Kelly had seen her from a distance at formal army events, but they'd never been introduced. As a lieutenant, she wouldn't normally socialize with a colonel's wife.

"Your table's ready, if you'd like to follow me," a waitress said.

They all trooped after the petite woman in a tiny black dress and white apron, through to what must once have been the next cottage before it was converted.

Stopping at a table in the corner by a huge Christmas tree, Kelly sat with a view out the tiny diamond panes of a leaded window towards the twinkling lights of Oxford.

"Cities always look better at night from a distance when all you can see are the lights," Alice said.

"I like Oxford," Olivia chimed in. "The shopping's good."

They both laughed and Kelly joined in. She already knew Alice and hoped Olivia would accept her as a friend as well. While the men chatted about surgery, Kelly took part in the baby chat with Alice and Olivia, really enjoying the female company. Hearing about the antics of Alice's little boy, Sami, and Olivia's two children was fun.

They ordered and were halfway through their meal when Alice stopped eating and screwed up her face. "The small of my back aches like mad. I've been trying to ignore it, but I can't anymore."

Cameron rubbed a soothing hand in circles over the painful place. "Perhaps we should go home, love."

"Yes. I think so. I just need to visit the ladies' room first. The baby likes to sit on my bladder." With Cameron's assistance, she heaved her heavy body out of the chair and straightened, a hand pressed against her lower spine.

"Shall I help?" Kelly stood, going to Alice's side to offer her arm.

Olivia followed. "I'll come as well."

Alice made her way between the tables, Kelly and Olivia at hand, ready to help if necessary. Just outside the restrooms, Alice leaned a shoulder against the wall, groaning. "My tummy and back really hurt now. I think the contractions must have started."

"Cam had better call the hospital. I'll get him," Olivia said.

Kelly went in the restroom with Alice and waited while she used the toilet. She came out and sat on the velvet bench, rubbing her belly.

"The pain is definitely coming in waves. I've done all the classes and I'm still not sure if they're contractions. What do you think?" She turned a questioning gaze on Kelly.

Kelly smiled weakly. "You'd best ask Olivia. I've never given birth." She was tempted to add that she never would. A sudden urge filled her to share her burden, but this was not the time or place. Alice had enough on her mind.

Kelly sat beside Alice and rubbed her lower back as Cameron had earlier. "Does that help?"

"Yes, thanks. If you like, you're welcome to come and see the baby as soon as he's born."

"I'd love to. I'm a sucker for kids, especially newborns."

"I remember how good you were with Sami when I was first admitted to the field hospital in Africa. I don't know what I'd have done without your help. I don't think I ever thanked you properly."

"No need. I was happy to lend a hand."

"I'm so pleased you hooked up with Sean. The two of you look good together. I hope it works out."

Kelly had always wondered if Cameron's wife knew of the soft spot she had for her husband. She had an inkling that she did.

"Thank you. I owe you one for getting me the bunny girl gig."

Alice laughed, then winced and pressed a palm to her belly. Kelly rubbed her back some more.

The restroom door opened and Olivia hurried in, Cameron on her heels. He rushed to Alice's side, put his arm around her, and helped her to her feet. "I've called the hospital. They're expecting us. We'll stop at home for your bag on the way."

"What about Sami?"

"Don't worry. Everything's arranged. Olivia and Radley will follow us and take him home with them."

"Good luck," Kelly said, pursuing them out.

Cameron smiled at her over his shoulder, a warm, friendly smile full of affection, a smile that triggered so many happy memories. "Thanks, Kell. Have a lovely Christmas with Sean."

Kelly stood at the open door of the pub, Sean's arm around her shoulders against the chill. Together they watched Cameron and Alice drive off, followed a few moments later by Radley and Olivia.

"Funny to think that by this time tomorrow there will likely be a new little Knight in the world," Sean said. "Nature's a wonderful thing."

"A Christmas baby." Kelly's sigh of longing spread a smoky plume through the cold air.

Chapter Eight

What a strange evening. In the quiet back of the taxi on the way home from dinner, Sean slid his hand over Kelly's and squeezed. The car passed along the narrow country lanes, the River Thames on their left, moonlight painting ripples of gold on the water.

"Are you all right, Kell?"

"Hmm." She didn't even look at him.

She seemed withdrawn, almost sad; he had no idea why. His instinct was to take her in his arms to comfort her, but he wasn't sure that's what she'd want. They'd both been happy after the visit to Santa with the girls. He'd hoped the date would go well and bring them even closer.

He'd been resisting the temptation of Kelly ever since the night he met her at his birthday party. In the end, his rule of not dating women he worked with or employed had fallen by the wayside.

And he was glad. After a year in an emotional desert, he had found an oasis. These last two weeks he felt as though he'd been poised on the edge, too scared to take the leap and try love again.

Staring at Kelly's profile in the dim light, he realized he'd already leaped the first time he kissed her. Now he was falling. If he didn't trust her to catch him, he was going to hit the ground with an almighty painful thud when she left.

The twins had formed a strong attachment to Kelly as well. Monique was supposed to provide female company for them, but she would never be anything more than an employee.

Did he want his girls raised by an employee? No. He wanted them to have a mother, to experience the love and stability of a proper family. It was time to let the past go. Eleanor had done her best to make him miserable, but he wouldn't allow her continue to rule his life.

Kelly was everything Eleanor hadn't been—kind, thoughtful, caring, and loving. She filled his dreams at night and his thoughts during the day, even though he tried to banish her and concentrate on his work. She had woken his libido and reminded him that he was missing a loving woman in his arms.

Tonight it was time to trust this woman who had moved into his house and stolen his heart, and share all he had to give.

The taxi turned through the open gates to River View House and stopped outside the front door. Sean pulled some money from his wallet and handed it to the driver. "Can you take the babysitter home? It's only a couple of miles down the road."

The man nodded. "Sure thing. Thanks, mate."

The cold air hit Sean's face as he climbed from the vehicle, but his blood surged hot through his veins in anticipation.

Kelly waited for Sean to round the car and open her door, then stepped out and accepted his arm to walk to the house. A strange melancholy had fallen over her when Alice and Cameron left for the hospital, as if this baby of Cameron's marked the end of an era. Really, the end of the era had come over a year ago when Cameron married Alice.

It wasn't that Kelly wanted to go back in time and have Cameron for herself again. She simply wished for a chance to relive those early hopes and dreams, the promise for the future she'd felt when she and Cameron dated during his first posting in Germany.

They'd been young and innocent then, before they were stationed in a war zone, before she found out she couldn't have children.

"You're very quiet." Sean curved his arm around her back as he unlocked the front door.

"Just thinking."

He smiled and stepped aside for her to enter first. The sound of the television blared from the sitting room. She couldn't face watching the babysitter flirt with Sean right now. She felt old and world-weary. "I'll go and check the girls. Will you send Lisa home?"

"Okay. I won't be long."

Sean strode along the hall towards the kitchen and Kelly mounted the stairs. She paused just inside the door to the babies' bedroom, listening to the soft sound of their breathing.

Both girls slept peacefully. Kelly adjusted Annabelle's covers, then gently touched the cute curl that fell across Zoe's forehead. They might be identical twins but she could tell them apart easily. They were so different in personality and behavior, each one a little darling in her own way.

Much as she enjoyed being with Sean and looked forward to dating him, the girls each held a corner of her heart as well. She had fallen in love with all three members of the Fabian family.

Voices sounded downstairs, then the front door closed, followed by the familiar tread of Sean's footsteps on the stairs.

"All okay?" he asked from the doorway. The hall light silhouetted the masculine outline of his broad shoulders and narrow hips, shooting a burst of longing through her.

Longing that might be doomed to remain unfulfilled.

A relationship with a man who already had children sounded like the answer to her prayers. The trouble was Sean's first wife had left him with such painful baggage, he might never be ready to move on.

She stepped aside as Sean moved to peep at Annabelle and Zoe. "They look peaceful."

She nodded.

"Are you sure you're okay, Kell?" Sean grasped her fingers and brushed his lips across her palm. Streamers of sensation ran up her arm. Every time he touched her, nerves sparked beneath her skin like fireworks.

Drawing her closer, he stroked a hand up her back to caress her hair. "It's thirty minutes until Christmas Day."

She followed his gaze to the illuminated clock on the nursery wall. "So it is. After the drama with Alice, I'd nearly forgotten it was Christmas."

"I hadn't." He grinned, those sexy dimples appearing on his cheeks.

He took her hand and tugged her out onto the landing, a mischievous twinkle in his eyes.

"What's going on?" He definitely had something on his mind.

Holding both her hands, he backed up, taking her with him towards his bedroom door. He stopped outside and pulled her into his arms. She splayed her palms on his chest, felt the firm contours of muscles beneath his shirt. Her gaze met his, her whole body tingling.

"I want to make love with you, Kelly."

The teasing look on his face was gone, an intensity of need in his eyes.

She trembled inside, excited but nervous of taking this step, and risking her heart. "You do realize that technically tonight was only our first date?"

"Let's not get bogged down in technicalities. I prefer to follow my instincts. Right now my instincts know exactly what I want. You."

He lowered his mouth to hers. Kelly melted in his arms at the smooth, warm brush of his lips. The gentle caress of his hands wiped away all thought. Her instincts knew what she wanted as well.

Happiness flooded Sean's senses the moment he woke to the sweet floral fragrance of Kelly. She was still here, in his bed. Last night was not a dream. He hadn't realized how lonely he'd been until this wonderful woman came into his life.

He rolled on his side and watched her sleep, her dark red hair spread across the pillow, wild and thick. He'd never known a woman with hair like hers. She had so much of it. In contrast, the rest of her features were neat and small. Her dark lashes lay in perfect crescents against her cheeks, her upper lip a bow, her bottom lip soft, full, and, as he'd discovered last night, very bitable.

She'd loved him with a passion and energy that left him breathless.

He gently stroked some hair away from her face so he could see her better. A faint sigh whispered between her lips and her eyelashes fluttered in her sleep. Dreaming of him? He hoped so.

Why had he ever thought that dating her would be enough? He wanted this woman in his life full time, living in his home, and sleeping in his bed. She was so unlike Eleanor it was as though they were different species. She would never lie to him, deceive him, or hurt him as Eleanor had.

Sean trusted Kelly with the most precious things in his life, his sweet angels, Zoe and Annabelle. He could trust her with his heart as well.

He watched her for a while as the wintry sun fought back the lingering darkness and light filtered into the room. He grew impatient to talk to her and wanted her to wake up. They only had a week left before the New Year. After that he was due back at work, unless he extended his leave. He didn't want to waste a moment of their time together.

She stirred and he took the opportunity to pull her into the curve of his body. With a murmur, she came to him all soft, sleepy, and adorable.

"Sean," she whispered.

He snuggled her closer, relishing the slide of her skin on his. "Merry Christmas, darling."

Her eyes blinked open and she rubbed them. "Are the girls awake?"

"Not yet."

A slow smile spread across her face. She wriggled against him, making his breath catch in desire. "Merry Christmas to you too. Has Santa remembered to put the girls' presents under the Christmas tree?"

"Santa might have been too busy last night enjoying himself to think of that. He'll do it in a little while." Sean was not about to leave her arms to lay out gifts. There would be plenty of time for that later. Right now he wanted to be with Kelly. His instincts demanded he make love to her again, but while they had no other distractions he needed to talk to her, to let her know exactly how he felt.

Kelly stretched, arching her body against Sean's in a dreamy, semiconscious daze. She loved this man, loved everything about him. He was kind, generous and caring, the sort of man any woman would be lucky to share her life with. The fact he had the face of an angel and the body of a Greek god didn't hurt either.

In the heat of the moment last night, she had nearly blurted that she loved him but held back, frightened of scaring him off. After all, he'd said he wanted to take things slowly. But she'd fallen into the trap of hiding her feelings before. She'd spent years loving Cameron without telling him. She wasn't going to make the same mistake again.

She stroked a hand through his mussed hair and across the rough stubble on his jaw. She loved him in his army uniform all polished without a hair out of place, and she loved him just as much all ruffled and naked in bed.

He caught her hand and pressed a kiss to her palm. The long, tapered fingers of his clever hands stroked her skin, fingers so skilled with fine surgical work, and so skilled at bringing her pleasure.

He kissed the tip of her nose, her cheeks, and her lips, lingering over the last. When he pulled back, he smiled. "I've changed my mind," he said. "I'd like you to stay here if you want to."

Kelly's heart jolted. "As in...live with you?"

"I love having you here, Kell. I know I wanted to take things slowly and date, but we're already way past that stage."

Relief burst through Kelly so potent it was almost painful.

"I love you," she whispered. "I know we've only known each other a short while, but I do."

She met his intense blue gaze. Waiting, hoping he might return her feelings.

"It *has* only been a short while, but when you know, you know. I love you too." He hugged her so tightly she could hardly breathe.

For long moments they simply held each other, heart to heart, skin to skin. She pressed against him, wanting to melt into him so they never had to be apart.

"So you'll stay?" he said.

"How could you doubt it?"

"I hoped I hadn't put you off. I was overthinking

things, letting my past dictate my future."

"I forgive you." She tapped him on the end of his nose as he sometimes did to her, and he laughed.

"We make a good team caring for the children."

"We do."

"I don't expect you to do all the child care and household tasks, though. I know you want to continue nursing."

"Let me think about it. I love looking after the girls." At this moment, Kelly couldn't get her thoughts in order to make any decisions. Her heart danced, happiness bubbling inside her like a bottle of champagne ready to pop its cork. Then she remembered the au pair.

"What about Monique?" Kelly didn't want to put anyone out of a job, but the prospect of an au pair living with them 24/7 was not appealing.

"Monique thought she might have to stay in France to care for her grandmother. I'll give her a call tomorrow and tell her my plans. I'm sure she won't mind."

A sleepy murmur issued from the baby monitor on the nightstand, followed by soft chattering.

"Annabelle, I bet," Kelly said.

Sean nodded. "Looks like it's time to get up."

Much as Kelly loved being curled in bed with Sean, she was looking forward to seeing the girls. This would be a wonderful Christmas Day, her first Christmas playing mum to this family she hoped might one day really be hers.

Chapter Nine

Kelly put the turkey in the oven and started making the stuffing, humming along to the Christmas carols on the radio. Childish giggles and Sean's laughter kept pulling her gaze over her shoulder to where he played with his daughters on the thick rug in front of the fire.

He lay on his back as the two little girls jumped on him, squealing with excitement. Kelly wiped off her hands, grabbed her mobile phone, and snapped a few pictures of the family fun.

It still hadn't quite sunk in that Sean wanted her to stay on, to live with him. During the next week they could discuss the arrangements, but not today. Christmas Day was a time for carefree fun. The children had the right idea.

She and Sean had decided the girls should spread out opening their presents over the day so they didn't get overexcited. After breakfast they unwrapped a plastic play kitchen with an oven, sink, pans, and utensils. They didn't really know what to do with it yet, but they enjoyed chewing on the plastic vegetables and hitting Sean with the pans.

Sean left them playing in the large cardboard box the toy had come in, and joined Kelly in the kitchen. "What can I do to help?"

Kelly pointed at the potatoes. "Peel those if you like,

but you don't have to. I want you to enjoy yourself with the girls."

He stepped behind her, circled his arms around her waist, and kissed her neck, making her go all tickly. "I want you to enjoy yourself too. So let me help with lunch, then we can both relax."

They prepared the vegetables and trimmings, sipping glasses of wine, and laughing together at the children's antics. For the first time in her adult life, she was part of a family. Memories of her childhood swirled back, of the happy times with her parents and sister. She rarely saw them now they lived in Australia. Her mum and dad had emigrated to be near their grandchildren after Kelly's sister, Joanne, married an Aussie.

Kelly had flown down to spend Christmas with them a few years ago when she had leave from the army. The experience had been uncomfortable, everyone handling her with kid gloves. Her family had changed how they behaved around her once they knew she couldn't have children, as if every mention of her nephew and nieces would upset her. That was partly why she preferred not to tell people about her issue.

Thinking of her parents made Kelly pause and pull the mobile phone from her jeans pocket. She scrolled through the numbers to find that of her sister's place where her Mum and Dad would be on Christmas Day. Australia was ten hours ahead of the UK, so if she intended to wish them Merry Christmas, she needed to do it now.

"Going to make a call?" Sean asked.

"Yeah. I'll just speak to Mum and Dad quickly."

She wandered along the hall to the back door and stepped outside as she dialed. Her sister, Joanne, answered.

"Hi, Jo. It's Kelly. Just called to say Merry Christmas."

"Back at you, girl. It's great to hear from you. Why didn't you fly out to see us? I thought you had leave this Christmas."

Guilt whispered through Kelly and she shoved it aside. "I'm helping a friend look after his children."

"Is he good-looking?"

"Actually, yes."

"Then I forgive you. Mum's just come inside. She wants a chat."

"Merry Christmas, Mum."

While Kelly talked to her mother, she kicked ice off the step outside the back door, imagining her mum, dad and sister basking in the Australian sun.

"Okay, well, I'd better go."

"Maybe we'll see you in the New Year," her mother said hopefully.

"Maybe." As Kelly cut the connection, she sighed. She was going to be far too busy to make a trip to the other side of the world.

As she wandered back to the living room ready to join the girls to unwrap another present, the doorbell rang.

"I'll give you one guess who that is," Sean said.

"Your brother?"

Sean nodded.

"Did he talk to you about joining the army?"

"He called while I was at the hospital on Christmas Eve. I don't know what he's decided, though." Sean lifted his eyebrows and went to answer the door.

Daniel sauntered in grinning, a bag of presents in his hand. He leaned over the kitchen island to kiss Kelly's cheek. "Merry Christmas. Where are my lovely little nieces?" He spotted them playing and crouched as they toddled towards him, both squealing with excitement. They obviously knew who he was and liked him.

"Zoe and Belles, my Christmas babies. Uncle Dan

has presents for you. I know how much girls like presents."

"We're rationing presents," Sean said, following his brother back.

"Rationing presents. That's not the Christmas spirit. What a mean old daddy you have." He grinned at Sean as he put an arm around each baby and nuzzled their cheeks until they giggled.

"So, are you joining us for lunch?" Kelly asked.

"If you'll have me. I'm persona non grata at home. I told Dad I wanted to leave the practice yesterday evening." Daniel gave Sean an apologetic smile. "He blames you for turning the head of this gullible boy, by the way. He thinks you talked me into joining the army."

Sean shrugged and grabbed a wineglass from the cupboard. "He hasn't spoken to me for months anyway. I called to speak to Mum yesterday morning and he hung up on me. Want a glass of wine?"

"Why not. It started snowing as I arrived, so I won't be driving home. A tiny sprinkling of snow and my car skids around like a snowboard."

They all turned and stared out the wall of windows along the river frontage. Fat snowflakes tumbled out of the sky to cover the decking in a white fluffy coat.

Kelly picked Annabelle up and wandered to the window, pointing up at the sky. "Do you see the white stuff falling? That's snow. It's very cold but lots of fun to play with." Kelly unlatched the window in front of her and scraped a bunch of fresh snow into her hand.

Annabelle stuck her fingers in the white mush, squealed, and shoved a handful in her mouth. Zoe toddled over to join them and Kelly crouched to show the other twin. Zoe touched the snow warily before wiping her hand on her clothes.

After a sumptuous turkey dinner, the adults sat on the

sofa with the babies climbing across their laps, and handed out presents.

Kelly unwrapped a pretty heart-shaped pendant from Sean. He fastened it around her neck and kissed her. "Sorry it's not very exciting. I didn't have long to choose."

"It's beautiful." She had only bought him a sweater, not knowing what else to get.

A little after four, the phone rang. Sean picked it up and wandered to the window, staring out at the deepening snow.

"A boy! Congratulations. I'll tell Kelly. See you soon."

Kelly rose, her heart thumping. "Alice has had her baby?"

"Yes, this morning. Cam said we can go and visit if we want."

"I'd love to."

"I'll babysit." Both girls were crawling over Daniel with chocolate around their mouths. He didn't seem to mind and obviously adored them.

"Right. That's settled then. You know where the clean diapers are if you need them." Sean slapped his brother on the back with a grin.

"Not going to happen, mate," Daniel answered. He winked at Kelly as she kissed both babies before hurrying to put on her coat.

The snow was a few inches thick, but not a problem for the SUV. By the time they arrived at the hospital, darkness had fallen.

Sean stopped in his private parking space close to the entrance and they went up to the maternity level.

"Merry Christmas, sir," a nurse said.

"Happy holidays, Colonel Fabian." A young doctor gave Sean a thumbs-up as he stepped out of the elevator.

Sean smiled politely and greeted his colleagues.

A nurse directed them to Alice's room. She sat propped up in bed against some pillows, a tiny bundle in her arms.

"Oh, Alice." Tears pricked Kelly's eyes as she rushed to the bedside and gazed down at the newborn's sweet little face. "He's lovely."

"He's definitely a Knight. Look at all the dark hair." Alice kissed the baby's fluffy topknot.

Cameron came in with a drink for Alice and put it on the side table. "What do you think of Harry Knight?"

"He's adorable, Cam. Congratulations. I'm so happy for you." She hugged her dear friend, poignant tears overflowing her eyes. She was delighted to see him and Alice together with their new baby.

"Would you like to hold him?" Alice said.

"Oh, yes please, if you don't mind."

"I know how much you love babies. I remember when I arrived at the field hospital with Sami. You were over the moon to take him off my hands while I had my operation."

Alice held out her baby. Kelly lifted the tiny boy from her arms, cradling him against her chest, her breath tight in her lungs. His little eyes opened and he stared at her. "Hello, you darling boy."

Sean stepped close and wrapped his arm around her waist, squeezing gently. "He looks like you, Cam," he said.

She imagined holding her own baby boy, one with blond hair and blue eyes like the man at her side. Longing as sharp and painful as shards of glass pierced her heart.

Sean had held his two girls as newborns and enjoyed this stage of fatherhood. He had his family. By staying with him, she wasn't depriving him of this. Her breath eased but the pain still stabbed her chest. Whatever she told herself, she would give anything to have her own baby.

"Thank you for letting me hold him. He's a little angel. You're very lucky." She passed tiny Harry Knight across to his proud father and they chatted for a few minutes, then she and Sean left the new parents in peace to enjoy their baby.

Sean gripped her hand as they crossed the marble and stainless steel hospital foyer and stepped out into the chilly air. Flakes of snow spiraled down from the dark sky, hitting her in the face as she angled her head up.

They crunched across the icy car park and Sean opened the SUV door for her to climb in. When he joined her, he turned up the heater to warm the vehicle.

"You're quiet again, Kell. Something upsets you about Alice's baby?"

"Gosh, no. I'm thrilled for them. I'm just a little tired, that's all." She wasn't looking forward to telling Sean that she couldn't have children. If they were in a relationship he deserved to know, but not yet. She didn't want to spoil Christmas Day for them both.

Sean turned the radio to a channel playing Christmas songs and drove off, humming along. "You know, I'd love to have a baby boy one day, a brother for Zoe and Annabelle," he said thoughtfully.

Kelly froze. She gripped the seat belt, digging her nails in the fabric as pain knotted her gut. She didn't want to deprive him of another baby if he really wanted one, but he did have two girls. Why couldn't that be enough?

She was so absorbed in her thoughts she didn't notice Sean staring at her. "You're worrying me, Kell. Tell me what's the matter so I can help."

The wipers swiped away snowflakes, beating rhythmically while Bing Crosby crooned "White Christmas."

There was no gentle way to say this, no easing into the subject. "I should have told you before. I can't have children."

"Are you sure? There're lots of treatments for infertility these days."

"There's no treatment for a hysterectomy. I had endometrial cancer when I was twenty-three."

"Aw hell, I'm sorry." Sean scraped a hand back through his hair. He stopped at a road junction on a quiet country lane, leaned over, and pulled her into his arms. "My poor love. Sorry if I sounded insensitive. I should have thought before I spoke."

Nausea clenched Kelly's stomach. Was he going to make a big thing out of this like her family had? Once people knew about her problem, they treated her differently. "It's okay. You didn't know. It was a long time ago. Let's just forget about it."

"Is there any risk of the cancer returning?"

Kelly wriggled out of his arms and sat back to get some space. "No. Can we leave the subject alone? It's not really something I want to discuss at Christmas. Today's supposed to be relaxing."

"Okay." His troubled gaze lingered on her face and she stared out the windshield, willing him to drive on.

"Look, my comment about wanting another baby was just a throwaway thought after seeing Cameron's son. I'm happy with my two girls, honestly."

The sick tension in her belly tightened. Was he only saying that because he now knew her medical history or did he really mean it?

He grasped her clenched fingers in her lap and stroked gently. "We'll say no more about it if you like."

"Thanks." Tension crawled up her back and gripped the muscles in her neck until her head ached. "I'm sorry I didn't tell you before."

"It's not an issue. Honestly." He rubbed a hand over his face. "Okay, well, I guess we'd better get home before my brother is forced to change a diaper." Sean drove on, the only sound the slashing windshield wipers.

Chapter Ten

Sean was losing Kelly and he didn't know what to do about it.

With a sinking sense of loss, he played with his babies on the sofa in the sitting room, helping them sort pictures of animals on the coffee table. Even though he chatted to them, most of his attention remained focused on Kelly as she prepared the children's lunch in the kitchen area.

Everything had gone wrong on the drive home from visiting Alice and the baby. After Kelly told him about her cancer and hysterectomy, she had transformed into a different woman.

She wouldn't discuss the subject and grew defensive and prickly when he mentioned it. He was worried about her, but she had shut him out. Every day she seemed to withdraw further into herself, tensing when he touched her. She'd even changed how she behaved with the children.

The happy, easy-going woman he knew had disappeared. He wouldn't have believed it possible if he hadn't seen it with his own eyes. The final straw came yesterday when she caught him researching endometrial cancer. She had been furious and retreated to her bedroom, slamming the door.

He walked on eggshells around her now, never

knowing when he opened his mouth if she would take offense.

She obviously hadn't come to terms with the past. But if she wouldn't talk about it, what could he do? He only wanted to help her. He loved her.

"The girls' lunch is ready," she called.

He dragged himself out of his miserable thoughts. "Come on, you two. Time to fill those tummies."

Sean pasted on a smile and led his daughters by their hands through to the table. He lifted them into their high chairs one at a time before fastening the safety straps.

Kelly put a bowl of chicken and vegetables in front of each girl, then sat between them with a wet cloth, ready to wipe faces and hands.

"We'll eat shortly," she said. "Our sausage pie is still in the oven."

"Sounds great." Sean bent to kiss the top of her head. She tensed and didn't turn to put her arms around him as she used to. Her ramrod spine sent out a clear message—go away and leave me alone.

He gripped the back of his neck, at a loss to know how to mend things between them. "Are you all right, Kell?"

Her breath hissed in and she cast him a narrow-eyed glare. "Will you please stop asking me that or I'll go crazy. Yes. I'm all right. Okay?"

"Okay." Sean had to get out of there and think. He took the stairs two at a time, and shut himself in his bedroom. Wrenching open the glass door, he stepped out on the balcony and paced back and forth. He drew in long draughts of cold air to calm his raging emotions and clear his head.

He didn't have enough experience with women to know how to handle this, but his brother did. Daniel had a new girlfriend every few weeks. Sean stepped back inside, grabbed his mobile phone from the nightstand, and scrolled through his contacts.

"Yo, Sean. How are you, mate?" Daniel answered.

"I've been better."

"Kelly?"

"Yep."

Daniel had witnessed the meltdown in Sean's relationship with Kelly the day after Christmas and made a hasty exit. "Kell seems so easygoing. I thought your tiff would have blown over by now."

"It hasn't. She didn't even come to bed with me last night. She had a headache." It hurt that she'd rather sleep alone than be with him. If she felt bad, he was happy just to cuddle and look after her.

"Buy her a present, the more expensive the better. Jewelry usually does the trick for me."

Sean closed his eyes and pinched the bridge of his nose. He should have realized the women Daniel dated were as shallow as puddles and nothing like Kelly. "I don't think something sparkly is going to fix this."

He could almost hear Daniel's shrug. "I like Kell, but no woman's worth this much hassle. Plenty more fish in the sea."

"Yeah. Thanks." For nothing. Sean cut the connection and rested his hands on the balcony railing, staring at the meltwater rushing past in the river below.

An expensive bauble would not win Kelly over. He needed something to pierce that damn wall she'd thrown up around herself to keep him out, something to make her understand he loved her and cared for her.

Then an idea occurred to him. There was one piece of jewelry that was bound to get through to her. His heart pounded at the scary prospect of making a commitment he had vowed never to repeat. But it was the only way to show Kelly how much he loved her. It didn't matter if she couldn't have children. He wanted to be with her. He'd do whatever it took to make sure she felt loved and appreciated, just as she was.

***

Sean wandered back into the kitchen as Kelly was taking the sausage pie out of the oven. She glanced at him, trying to gauge his mood. The anxious air of concern in his eyes made her grit her teeth. Why couldn't he forget about her cancer and treat her like he had before? This was exactly what had happened when she told her family—they fussed and tried to wrap her in cotton wool.

"Lunch will be on the table in a moment," she said, aiming for a light, breezy tone.

"I'm not really hungry yet. I'll run out for a while and have something to eat when I come back."

Kelly's gaze jumped from the plates she had pulled from the warmer to Sean's face. "Where are you going?"

"Just into Oxford."

She waited for him to elaborate but he didn't. "Okay."

"See you later." He dropped a kiss on her cheek, said good-bye to the children, and headed out.

Kelly stared after him, her heart drumming. Why had he been so mysterious? Was he going out to get away from her? She'd noticed he'd spent less time with her since her revelation.

Maybe he'd had a rethink and decided he did want another baby. Perhaps she should do the decent thing and walk away like she had with Cameron, give Sean the opportunity to meet someone else who could have children.

Her relationship with Sean wasn't going to work out. She couldn't handle the way he fussed over her all the time. It was best if she went back to her original plan.

The charity job was still available. They were always short of qualified nurses with overseas experience. She would get tremendous satisfaction and fulfillment from working with the poor needy children in Somalia.

Kelly sat at the table alone and ate her sausage pie one slow mouthful at a time, the food tasting like sawdust. After struggling through half of it, she tossed the rest in the trash.

She carried the babies upstairs, then changed their diapers. Annabelle struggled and cried as Kelly laid her on the changing table. Even the children had become difficult over the last few days. They must be reacting to their father's strange mood.

A sigh wrenched from Kelly's chest as she finished with the fussy baby and changed Zoe. She'd felt as though she belonged here, yet after she told Sean her medical history, the happy family atmosphere had melted away with the snow. This was the last time she would ever tell anyone about her cancer and hysterectomy.

She fetched her laptop from her bedroom, sat cross-legged on the floor beside the babies, and fired off an e-mail to her contact at the charity. They were going to think she was schizophrenic; first she wanted to work overseas, then she didn't, now she did again.

The front door opened downstairs. Sean was back. Her heart leaped as excitement raced along her nerves, her instincts still not caught up with the change in their relationship. With a groan, she dropped her head in her hands. All she wanted to do was cry; instead she had to put on a brave face until she could leave.

"Kelly."

"In the nursery," she called back. "I'll be down in a moment." He probably wanted his lunch now.

Kelly shut her laptop, pushed herself up from the floor, and began the long task of helping the girls downstairs. They backed down on all fours so they didn't fall.

By the time they reached the kitchen, Sean had nearly finished the sausage pie she left on the counter for him. "Don't you want me to heat it up?"

"I popped it in the microwave."

"Oh. Right."

"This is tasty. A nice change from turkey leftovers."

"The turkey did seem to go on forever, didn't it?"

"Yep. We'll get a smaller one next year."

His words sent a jolt of hope through her. Was that just a turn of phrase, or did he really believe she would still be here next Christmas?

For the first time in a couple of days, she relaxed with Sean and smiled. He grinned back, the dimples she so loved appearing in his cheeks. She reached up and touched one, laughing when he grabbed her fingers and kissed them.

"Let's take the girls for a walk. It's nice outside, cold but clear and fresh."

"Okay, sounds good." They hadn't been out anywhere since the fateful trip to the hospital to see Alice and the baby.

Sean dashed upstairs, returning a few minutes later with the girls' all-in-one winter suits. He dressed Zoe while Kelly helped Annabelle suit up for the cold.

They carried the babies to the utility room and put them in their stroller before donning their own coats, scarves, and hats.

The crisp chill stung Kelly's cheeks as she stepped out of the warm house. The fresh air cleared her head and sharpened her thoughts. Birds swooped across the pale blue winter sky, and dead leaves fluttered on the ground as they set off along the riverside footpath.

"I needed to blow away the cobwebs," Sean said.

"Me too." Kelly walked on her own for a little while, then slipped her arm through Sean's as he pushed the stroller. He smiled at her, looking more like the man she had fallen in love with.

Then he had to spoil it. "Why did everything go wrong between us on Christmas Day?"

"Did it?"

"Come on, Kell. You know it did."

"Okay." She chewed her lip, not wanting to answer. Yet what did she have to lose? "One of the reasons I put off telling you about my hysterectomy was because I knew it would change how you treat me. I was right."

Sean's eyebrows rose. "I'm not the one who changed, you are. You've shut me out. I care about you, love. I want to be there for you, yet you won't talk to me."

Kelly pulled back her arm and halted. "I don't need any special treatment. Just treat me the same way you did before my confession."

"If you behaved how you used to, I could do that."

Kelly huffed with frustration. He was just like her family.

Sean parked the stroller beside a wooden bench and snapped on the brake. The babies were both asleep, huddled in their warm winter suits.

"Will you sit with me for a moment?"

Kelly plopped down on the bench, her shoulders aching with tension.

"I have a present for you."

"You've already given me something for Christmas."

"I know. This is an extra present. A special one."

He pulled a small box from his coat pocket wrapped in gold and tied with a gauzy silver ribbon.

Kelly's heart fluttered and leaped, her gaze rising from the gift to his face. He smiled, the warm affection in his blue eyes calming her fears like a soothing hand.

With a racing pulse, she took the gift and pulled away the paper to reveal a red velvet box. "More jewelry?" She cast a questioning glance his way.

"Open it and find out."

She raised the box lid to reveal a huge solitaire diamond ring. Her fluttering heart nearly burst from her chest. She pressed a hand over her ribs, struggling to draw breath.

"Is this a..."

"An engagement ring. Yes. It's the only way I could think of to prove I love you. You can shut me out and push me away all you like, but I'm not giving up on you. I don't want to lose you, Kell."

Tears pricked Kelly's eyes and stung her nose. She pressed her lips together tightly until the need to cry receded. Sean pulled off his glove and curved a warm palm around her cheek.

"Will you marry me, Kelly? Be my wife and mother to Zoe and Annabelle. We all love you and want you to stay with us."

Tears overflowed her lashes and ran down her cheeks. "I thought you didn't want me anymore."

He grunted with frustration and pulled her into his arms. "Of course I want you. I wish I'd never made that stupid comment about another baby. I want you, Kelly Grace. If down the line we decide we'd like another child, we can always adopt."

"You told me you wouldn't get married again." Kelly's words tumbled out in a blubbering muddle with her tears.

"I'm allowed to change my mind, aren't I?"

"Yes."

"Good." He stroked the hair away from her face where it was sticking to her wet cheeks. "You haven't answered me yet."

"Yes. I want to marry you."

"Wonderful." Sean dragged her onto his lap and rocked her, kissing away her tears. Kelly kissed him back, passion and desire flaring inside her. How she adored this kind, loving man who was willing to accept her with all her faults.

He knew her deepest, darkest secret, yet he still wanted her. Relief seared along her nerves and set her pulse racing as she curled against him. Framing his dear face between her hands, she smothered him in tiny kisses, making him laugh.

For so long she had dreamed of having her own children and he was giving her that dream. She would be the happiest wife and mother in the world with two adorable little daughters and the handsomest husband ever.

Epilogue

Kelly laughed with anticipation as she jumped out of the rental car outside her sister's house in Perth. She and Sean had left the cold temperatures of England to celebrate the New Year under the hot sun and blue skies of Australia.

"You go on ahead," Sean said to her. "I'll get the girls out."

"Yay, Kelly!" Joanne burst through her front door and dashed down the path to meet Kelly as she opened the gate. They hugged for a long time, the years melting away as if they had seen each other only yesterday. "It's been too long, you dirty stay-away."

"It was you who moved to the opposite end of the world."

"Darling, you're here." Kelly's mum and dad hurried out and grabbed her for hugs.

She held on to her mum for a long time, blinking back tears at the sight of all the gray in her mum's hair. The years had whizzed past. If it hadn't been for Sean, she might not have come to see her parents again.

"So, where's this fiancé of yours?" her father said.

Sean appeared at the gate with a little girl clutching each hand and the changing bag over his shoulder. He gave a crooked grin, his golden hair gleaming in the sun, his eyes as blue as the Indian Ocean shimmering in the distance.

"Holy cow." Joanne gaped at Sean. "Where on earth did you find him and does he have a brother?"

"You're married, Jo." Kelly smacked her sister's arm.

Sean shook her father's hand and politely swapped hugs and kisses with her mother and sister.

"How absolutely adorable." Her mother leaned down to see Zoe and Annabelle. "You two darlings are the prettiest twins I've ever seen."

"Come on in. The kids are out back with Eric. We're going to eat outside on the deck by the pool." Joanne turned a bright smile on Kelly. "We've cooked a New Year's turkey since you missed Christmas with us."

Kelly met Sean's gaze. He gave her a wry grin. Neither said they had already eaten enough turkey this Christmas to last them all year.

"Sounds great," Kelly said. "Lead on."

She lifted Zoe into her arms while Sean picked up Annabelle. Both babies had slept for much of the time on the second leg of their flight, after a twenty-four hour stopover in Singapore.

They walked through the house and emerged into the grassy backyard. Luxuriant shrubs covered in bunches of golden blooms and red spiky bottlebrush flowers bordered the deck. The sun blazed down. It was a shock to the system after leaving an icy UK.

Kelly was relieved to step under the shady canopy over the table. A Christmas tablecloth and a fat gold candle surrounded by plastic holly sprigs gave a festive touch to the dinner setting.

On the corner of the deck, a traditional Christmas tree blinked with lights and sparkled with baubles. "It seems so weird having Christmas in the summer," Kelly said.

"I know. I long for snow sometimes. Not for long, though." Joanne gazed across the garden and raised her voice. "Marty, Tina, Niki. Come here, you three. Say hello to your auntie Kelly."

A dark-haired boy of six and two little girls of four and three dashed across the lawn from where they were playing in the swimming pool to give Kelly wet hugs.

Fresh tears filled her eyes to see her nieces and nephew. The last time she visited here, Marty had been two, and the girls hadn't been born. She had only seen photographs of them.

"It's wonderful to meet you all." She sat with Zoe in her arms and Sean crouched at her side, holding Annabelle. "Say hello to Zoe and Belles." The children were so cute all hugging each other.

"Hi there." Joanne's husband carried out the turkey and set it on the table before shaking Sean's hand and kissing Kelly. They took their seats, Kelly's mother claiming Zoe to sit on her lap.

"Oh, Kelly, they're adorable. You're a very lucky girl." Her mother threw an arm around her shoulders, pressing her cheek to Kelly's. "I'm so happy for you, darling, and thrilled that you found the time to come all this way to see us."

"I won't leave it so long next time, Mum."

"That's all right, sweetheart. All that matters is you're here now and you're happy."

"I am. Really happy. Sean is wonderful."

She held out her left hand to show off her ring before gripping Sean's fingers. His gaze met hers, the corners of his lips lifting in an affectionate smile, his eyes alight with pleasure.

"I love you, darling," she said, leaning close to kiss him. This man hadn't just welcomed her into his family, he'd helped her find her own family again, encouraged her to take a chance and come to Australia to reconnect with her parents and sister. Now that she was here, she couldn't understand why she had stayed away so long.

"I love you too," he said.

"Love, love, love, love," Annabelle chanted and Zoe joined in.

Everybody burst out laughing.

"Yes, we do love, love, love." Kelly kissed both her adorable babies and their wonderful daddy. She had been blessed with the very best Christmas present in the world, a family to love.

The Army Doctor's Baby

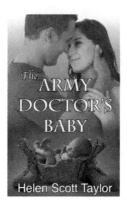

After his wife betrayed him, Major Radley Knight dedicated himself to becoming the best Army doctor he could be, dedicated himself to saving soldiers' lives. When he returns on leave from Afghanistan he is ready for a break. Instead he finds himself helping a young mother and her newborn baby. He falls in love with Olivia and her sweet baby boy and longs to spend the rest of his life caring for them. But Olivia and her baby belong to Radley's brother.

Praise for The Army Doctor's Baby

"This is a sweet romance with a wonderful happily ever after. Highly recommend this read!" Luvbooks

"I loved this sweet, tender romance about a woman in need of a father for her baby and the man who falls in love with her..." Ruth Glick

"Loved the twists at the end of the book. Just the right amount of tension to keep me turning those pages! Totally recommend." Mary Leo

The Army Doctor's Wedding

Major Cameron Knight thrives on the danger of front-line battlefield medicine. Throwing himself into saving the lives of injured servicemen keeps the demons from his past away. When he rescues charity worker, Alice Conway, and a tiny newborn baby, he longs for a second chance to do the right thing, even if it means marrying a woman he barely knows so they can take the orphan baby to England for surgery. The brave, beautiful young woman and the orphan baby steal his heart. He wants to make the marriage real, but being married to an army officer who's stationed overseas might do her more harm than good.

Praise for The Army Doctor's Wedding

"Grab a Kleenex because you are going to need it! This is one no romance lover should miss!" Teresa Hughes

"The book starts out with lots of action and holds the reader's interest through to the end. It's a great read!" Sue E. Pennington

About the Author

Helen Scott Taylor won the American Title IV contest in 2008. Her winning book, The Magic Knot, was published in 2009 to critical acclaim, received a starred review from *Booklist*, and was a *Booklist* top ten romance for 2009. Since then, she has published other novels, novellas, and short stories in both the UK and USA.

Helen lives in South West England near Plymouth in Devon between the windswept expanse of Dartmoor and the rocky Atlantic coast. As well as her wonderful long-suffering husband, she shares her home with a Westie a Shih Tzu and an aristocratic chocolate-shaded-silver-burmilla cat who rules the household with a velvet paw. She believes that deep within everyone, there's a little magic.

Find Helen at:
http://www.HelenScottTaylor.com
http://twitter.com/helenscotttaylo
http://facebook.com/helenscotttaylor
www.facebook.com/HelenScottTaylorAuthor

Book List

Paranormal/Fantasy Romance

The Magic Knot
The Phoenix Charm
The Ruby Kiss
The Feast of Beauty
Warriors of Ra
A Clockwork Fairytale
Ice Gods
Cursed Kiss

Contemporary Romance

The Army Doctor's Baby
The Army Doctor's Wedding
Unbreak My Heart
Oceans Between Us
Finally Home
A Family for Christmas
A Family Forever
Moments of Gold
Flowers on the water

Young Adult

Wildwood

Printed in Great Britain
by Amazon